"You are my wife! Do you understand?"

"No, dammit, I do not understand!"

"There's no time for explanations. Just do as you're told."

"Why?" Dorian's eyes flashed green sparks. "Because that's how the men of your country treat their women?"

Jake's eyes narrowed. "That's as good a reason as any."

"Well, I have news for you, Jake Prince. You may belong in this part of the world but I don't. And I am not your woman! I—"

She cried out as he reached for her and pulled her into his arms. His mouth dropped to hers and he kissed her with a harsh, unforgiving passion that left her breathless.

SANDRA MARTON has always believed in the magic of storytelling and the joy of living happily ever after with that special someone. She wrote her first romantic story when she was nine, and fell madly in love at sixteen with the man she would eventually marry. Today, after raising two sons and an assortment of furry, four-legged creatures, Sandra and her husband live in a house on a hilltop in a quiet corner of Connecticut.

Books by Sandra Marton

HARLEQUIN PRESENTS
1457—LOST IN A DREAM
1574—ROARKE'S KINGDOM
1637—THE CORSICAN GAMBIT
1736—A WOMAN ACCUSED

Don't miss any of our special offers. Write to us at the following address for information on our newest releases.

Harlequin Reader Service
U.S.: 3010 Walden Ave., P.O. Box 1325, Buffalo, NY 14269
Canadian: P.O. Box 609, Fort Erie, Ont. L2A 5X3

SANDRA MARTON

A Bride for the Taking

Harlequin Books

TORONTO • NEW YORK • LONDON
AMSTERDAM • PARIS • SYDNEY • HAMBURG
STOCKHOLM • ATHENS • TOKYO • MILAN
MADRID • WARSAW • BUDAPEST • AUCKLAND

ISBN 0-373-11751-5

A BRIDE FOR THE TAKING

Copyright © 1992 by Sandra Myles.

First North American Publication 1995.

Printed in U.S.A.

CHAPTER ONE

DORIAN had barely settled into the back of the taxi, silently thanking whatever gods were responsible for finding her an empty cab during a rainy evening rush-hour in mid-Manhattan, when traffic came to a sudden halt.

She sat forward, looked out at the press of buses, cars, and trucks, then rapped sharply on the smeared glass partition that separated her from the driver.

'I've got a plane to make,' she said in the cool, don't-fool-with-me voice she'd learned worked best during the five years she'd lived in New York City.

The cabbie looked into his rear-view mirror and lifted his shoulders in an eloquent shrug.

'Is a mess, lady,' he said agreeably. 'I do best I can.'

Dorian sank back into the cracked vinyl seat. His best, she thought glumly, would not be good enough if they didn't get to Kennedy Airport within the next hour. The chartered flight to Barovnia would take off, leaving her behind.

The thought made her shudder. She was on the first decent assignment *WorldWeek* magazine had given her and, after almost two years of doing research for other reporters and little filler pieces without the coveted 'byline' every journalist dreamed of, she wasn't about to lose her chance of becoming a correspondent.

A horn blared behind them, the single sound immediately taken up by what seemed to be every other vehicle caught in the tangled snarl that filled Fifty-Seventh Street. Even Dorian's driver began to pound his fist on the horn, all the while muttering to himself in a tongue that bore no resemblance whatsoever to English.

Dorian muttered something too, short and succinct and not at all ladylike. The cabbie glanced into the mirror as if he'd heard her. We're in this together, the look on his face said, but that wasn't true at all. The meter was running, adding dollars to her growing frustration. He could sit here all night if he had to; at least he was earning his pay. Dorian wouldn't really begin to earn hers until she'd boarded that damned charter flight.

It would be on the apron by now, hatches open as the personal luggage of the entire Barovnian entourage was loaded aboard. The reporters themselves would travel light, but Dorian was sure the delegation would not—especially the man at the centre of it.

Jack Alexander, the wealthy and powerful head of the giant corporation that controlled Barovnian exports, would expect to travel in style—even though his destination was an isolated kingdom with one foot still planted in the ignorance and poverty of the Middle Ages. And now—now, if the newly crowned *abdhan* of Barovnia died ...

Dorian slid backwards as the taxi shot into a sudden opening in the traffic. Good! They were moving again—but only as far as the next corner. She groaned and rapped once more on the partition.

'I absolutely, positively *must* get to Kennedy by seven,' she said. 'Please. Can't you do something?'

The driver threw up his hands. 'Is no my fault, miss.'

That was the motto of the day, Dorian thought glumly as she sank back in her seat. Her boss had used the same words when he'd dumped her into the middle of this situation.

She had been intent on the story she was writing, her fingers doing their usual hunt-and-peck across her computer keyboard while she tried to stretch a forty-word filler piece about the Florida citrus crop into one hundred words of journalistic brilliance, when a bulky shadow loomed across her desk. She looked up and saw Walt Hemple standing beside her.

'Got to see you, babe,' he said around the cigar that was, as always, clamped between his teeth.

Dorian nodded and got to her feet, biting back the desire to tell him for what would probably be the thousandth time that her name wasn't 'babe'. There was no point to it—'babe' was Hemple's standard form of address for all the women staffers, a not-so-subtle reminder that, even if the law and a changed society required that *WorldWeek* employ female reporters, Walt Hemple didn't have to like it.

She followed him through the crowded newsroom to his office—a narrow cubicle perfumed with the noxious fumes of his cigar. Hemple elbowed past her, grunting as he settled into the old-fashioned swivel-chair behind his desk.

'Sit,' he said, but, as usual, there was no place to sit. Files, papers and old copies of *WorldWeek* were piled on the only other chair in the room.

Hemple folded his hands across his ample belly and looked at her.

'So,' he said after a moment, 'how's it going?'

She blinked. What kind of question was that? Hemple was not a man given to making small talk, especially not with staffers as far down the ladder as she.

'All right,' Dorian said cautiously. 'I'm just about done with——'

'What do you know about Barovnia?'

She blinked again. Barovnia. Barovnia. She knew the name, of course. It had been in the papers weeks before. *WorldWeek* had even done a piece on it.

'Not much,' she said, still cautiously. 'It's a country near the Black Sea——'

'A kingdom. A mountain kingdom in the Carpathians.'

She nodded. 'Right. I remember now. The Barovnian king died a couple of months ago, and——'

'They don't have a king. They have an *abdhan*.' Hemple grinned around his cigar. 'He's like a cross between God and Emperor of the World—an absolute monarch with the power of life and death over his people.'

Dorian nodded again. 'This is all very interesting,' she said carefully, 'but what——?'

'Read,' he said, shoving a sheet of paper across the desk.

She started to do as instructed, but Hemple clucked his tongue impatiently and snatched back the paper.

'It's an announcement from the Barovnian embassy,' he said. 'It just came over the wire. The *abdhan* may die. If he does, they'll be crowning a new one.'

'But it's a mistake. You just said the king died last month——'

'Jeez, babe, get it straight, will you? He's called an *abdhan*. How many times I got to tell you that?'

Dorian's eyes narrowed beneath their veil of dark lashes. Count to ten, she told herself, and don't say anything you'll regret.

'What I'm saying, Walt, is that this is old news. The *abdhan* had an accident a couple of months ago——'

'Having a massive coronary in your sleep after eighty-five years of being one of the world's last absolute rulers can hardly be classified as an accident, babe.'

'The bottom line is that the old man died and they replaced him, which means the wire-service story is wrong. Do you want me to phone them and——?'

'The story is one hundred per cent on the money. The old guy died, they crowned his successor——'

'Seref Baldov. Wasn't that his name?'

'Right. And yesterday there was some kind of tribal ceremony, something to do with horses. A mock battle, who the hell knows——?'

'A tribal ceremony?' Dorian couldn't quite keep the scorn from her voice. 'Hasn't anyone told these people we're on the threshold of the twenty-first century?'

Hemple's teeth showed in a smile. 'Exactly. Americans are planning a mission to Mars and the Barovnians still play at being Cossacks. Interesting point, isn't it?'

Dorian sighed. Now she knew where this was going. A heading danced before her eyes. COSSACKS AND COSMONAUTS. Well, something like that. It didn't matter because the piece she'd write wouldn't rate a title. Walt would want a filler, some human interest thing that could be tucked in to fill space on the bottom of a page.

'How many words? Fifty?' she asked. 'A hundred?'

'So this Baldov guy,' Hemple said, ignoring her, 'the new *abdhan*, fell from his horse. He hit his head and now it looks like he may not pull through.'

Dorian nodded. 'I get the picture—although frankly I don't know why *World Week's* readers should much care. Just because this little king of barbarians wants to play Mongol warrior——'

Hemple's brows drew together. 'You need to do your homework, babe. Barovnia may be backward, but it's got oil reserves that make the Arabs look like paupers, and minerals they can mine for the next thousand years—and if Baldov kicks the bucket it's also going to have a new *abdhan*.'

He didn't want a filler, she thought, he wanted an article. Not from her, of course—she'd only do the research. Someone with a name would be tapped to really write the piece.

'Interesting,' she said, trying to look as if it really were. 'OK. I'll put together what I can. How much time do I have?'

'Send me your first fifteen hundred words as soon as you can after touchdown.'

Dorian's heart gave a thump of excitement. Hemple had never sent her further than Newark on a story. Surely, he couldn't mean...

'Am I going somewhere?' she asked carefully.

'The Barovnian embassy's arranged to fly a planeload of reporters from the major media out tonight.'

Dorian swept the stack of magazines and papers into her arms and sank down in the chair.

'Are you sending me to Barovnia to cover this coronation?'

Hemple shoved a slim manila folder across his scarred desk-top. 'That's all the background the library could put together on such short notice. You can read it in the taxi on your way to the airport.'

A thousand questions were racing through Dorian's head, but there was one in particular that demanded an answer, even though only a fool would ask it.

'Walt?' She took a breath. 'It's not that I'm not——' She hesitated. Pick a word, she told herself, one that won't give away the fact that you want to leap into the air and whoop with joy. She cleared her throat. 'It's not that I'm not pleased with this assignment, but it occurs to me, we didn't send anybody to cover the last guy's coronation.'

Her boss nodded. 'Right.'

Dorian nodded, too. 'Well, then, why...?' She hesitated again, but it had to be said. 'Why now? And why has the Barovnian embassy offered to fly reporters in? I mean, why would they think we'd be interested?'

Hemple leaned forward. 'Does the name Jack Alexander mean anything to you?'

It took a few seconds to change gears. 'Yes,' she said after a moment. 'Sure. He's the head of Alexander International.'

'Uh-huh. The guy inherited millions, and he's racked up millions more on his own.' Hemple switched his cigar from one side of his mouth to the other. 'What else do you know?'

She frowned. *WorldWeek* had done a piece on the man once, when she'd first started at the magazine....

A look of disdain narrowed her mouth. 'Our article said he collects women almost as easily as he collects money—except he holds on to the money.'

Walt Hemple laughed. 'I don't think we put it quite like that but yeah, that was the general idea. Anything else?'

'No, I don't——' She nodded. 'He hates personal publicity. His women lined up to be interviewed, but we couldn't get a reporter past Alexander's door.'

'Not with questions about himself, no. Ask him about Alexander International, he talks. Ask him about Jack Alexander, he turns to stone.'

'Walt, I really don't understand. All this is interesting, but what's the point? If you're sending me to Barovnia, what's all this side-bar stuff about Alexander have to do with it?'

Hemple's chair groaned its displeasure as he tilted it forward and leaned across his desk.

'Alexander International should really be called Barovnian Exports. Sixty, sixty-five per cent of what it controls comes from there.'

'So?'

'So,' Hemple said, smiling slyly, 'it turns out that our pal, Mr Alexander, has been sitting on a secret, babe.' He paused dramatically. 'Mama was a Southern belle. But Daddy—Daddy was a Barovnian. A Barovnian of royal lineage, no less.'

It was Dorian's turn to lean forward. 'What do you mean?'

'I mean,' Hemple said with relish, 'that Jack Alexander was born Jaacov Alexandrei.' The sly smile came again. 'I mean that the guy's a product of the Virginia Military Academy, Harvard, and the Wharton

School of Business—and now it turns out that under that hand-tailored, three-piece suit beats the heart of the guy who may become the next *abdhan*.'

Dorian's green eyes opened wide with shock. 'What?'

'Alexander's gonna be on that plane, along with a handful of his business buddies—American advisers, the Press release calls them. How's that grab you, babe?'

It grabbed her. How could it not? It was the best kind of story, a reporter's dream, all the most basic human interest stuff combined with something as serious as oil and gold and international dollars.

'Are you sure?' Hemple nodded, and Dorian frowned. 'Wait a minute. If this is the same Jack Alexander, the one who's gun-shy of publicity, why's he taking a plane-load of reporters along with him to Barovnia?'

'The embassy made the arrangements, not him.' Hemple's eyelid dropped in a conspiratorial wink. 'And from what I've heard—on the QT, of course—Alexander made them wait until the last minute before he agreed to their plan. The guy's no dummy. There'd be no way to keep something like this off the front pages—he must figure the best way to handle things is to control the story inside Barovnia, where he's got the power, instead of having rumours leak out from the foreign embassies.'

Dorian nodded. It made sense. The only thing that didn't make sense was that this plum should be falling into her lap.

'Just think,' Hemple said, chuckling. 'All these years, companies have lived or died on this guy's say-so—and now it turns out that he may get that kind of power over people's lives. God, is that a story just waiting to be written, or isn't it?'

It was. Oh, it definitely was. But why was he giving it to her? Why?

'Here.' Hemple tossed an envelope across his desk. 'Everything you need is in there, including chits to sign for Accounting so you can take some cash with you—

which reminds me, I want you to hop downstairs and buy whatever you think you'll need. Clothes, make-up—you know what I mean. The plane leaves in two hours, so there's no time to go home and get your stuff.'

Dorian nodded. 'That's OK. All I'll need is a toothbrush and a change of...' She fell silent. *Whatever you'll need. Clothes, make-up. Make-up ...*

And suddenly it all fell into place.

'Walt.' Her voice trembled a little with anger; she had to clear her throat before she could continue. 'Walt,' she said, choosing her words with the greatest care, 'I'm grateful for this chance. You know I am.'

Her boss's expression gave nothing away. 'But?'

'But I'm not—I mean, I assume you haven't chosen me because I'm ... I certainly wouldn't want to think that—that ...'

'Because you're a woman. A good-looking woman. Is that what you're choking over saying?'

Dorian swallowed hard. 'Yes. No. I mean—dammit, Walt, is that the reason you picked me? Because you think Alexander will—will notice me?'

Hemple's beady eyes moved over her, assessing without personal interest her shiny cap of silvery blonde hair, her wide-set green eyes fringed by heavy, dark lashes, the small straight nose and full mouth.

'He'd have to be dead not to notice you, babe,' he said flatly.

Dorian flushed. She had no illusions about her looks. She was pretty, perhaps more than pretty, but it was nothing to do with her. She had inherited her beauty, she hadn't worked at it as she had at honing her reporting skills, and if she'd wanted to use her looks she'd have done so long ago. More than one city-room editor had made it clear that she could get ahead by going to bed—his bed, more specifically. She could even more easily have carved a career in TV news, where a pretty face went a lot further than ability.

But she hadn't done any of that. And she wasn't about to start now.

'Walt.' She straightened in her chair. 'I want this assignment very badly. But I'm not going to take it if you think—if you're assuming I'll trade on my—on my looks to get anything out of Alexander. I don't work that way.' Her head lifted until her eyes were boring into his. 'And you've absolutely no right to ask me to do something like that, either.'

Hemple's smile was bland. 'I sent you out to interview that librarian who hit the jackpot a few months ago. Why did I choose you, do you think?'

'That's not the same thing.'

'Because your résumé says you worked a year as a library assistant, babe. It was a good fit, the same as it made sense to send Joe Banks to interview that sky-diver once I knew Banks jumped out of airplanes, too.'

'Walt, it's different. You're asking me to——'

'I'm asking you to be what you are—a reporter and a looker, too.' He gave her a quick, hard smile. 'Unless you'd rather I handed this over to somebody else.'

Dorian had stared at her boss, hating him for putting her in this spot, hating herself for not being able to tell him what he could do with his assignment, almost hating herself for being a woman.

It had been as if Hemple had been able to read her mind. His smile had broadened until it threatened to dislodge the cigar, and that had been when he'd uttered the words that almost mirrored the ones the taxi driver had used.

'Why fight reality, babe? After all, it's not *my* fault you're a good-looking broad, is it?'

Dorian sighed as she remembered the smirk on his face as he'd spoken. Hemple was a pig, she thought as the taxi exited the Queens Midtown Tunnel and started along the highway, but he was the man in charge.

She took the file folder from her bag and opened it. The bottom line was that he'd given her an assignment, and she would fulfil it to the best of her ability.

She would certainly not use sex to accomplish it; she'd made that clear enough to him before she'd left his office. Hemple had only smiled. Dorian had known what he was thinking: that if Alexander had a choice between talking to her and to a male reporter he'd talk to her.

She sighed again as she began leafing through the papers inside the folder. Even if he did, it wouldn't be because she'd gone out of her way to set things up. Certainly, she'd done nothing to glamourise herself.

She'd taken money from Accounting and dashed to a little shop on the corner where she'd bought a large carrying bag and only the basics: comb, toothbrush, underwear, a pair of jeans and a couple of T-shirts in addition to the khaki trouser suit she was wearing. Nothing feminine, nothing——

There was a sudden bang and the taxi lurched sharply to the right. Dorian cried out as the papers in her lap went flying. The driver cursed, this time loudly and fluently in Anglo-Saxon English, and pulled the vehicle off the road and on to the grassy verge.

Dorian leaned forward and hammered on the partition. 'What happened?' she demanded. 'Why are we stopping?'

The man turned and slid the glass aside. 'We have flat tyre, miss. I must change.'

She stared at him. 'How long will that take?'

He shrugged. 'Ten minute. Maybe fifteen. It is raining. Not so easy to do.'

'Well, then—can you call for another taxi to come and pick me up?'

He shrugged again. 'Sure. Can do. But other car may not come any faster than I change tyre.'

Dorian glanced at her watch. 'Do it anyway, please,' she said. 'I'm really desperate.'

He did as she'd asked, then set to work. It had gone from afternoon to night now, and the rain had turned into a steady downpour. Time passed, but no new taxi appeared.

Dorian flung open the door and stepped out into the darkness. Wind buffeted her; she felt the rain drive straight through her thin cotton jacket and trousers, felt it plaster her hair to her skull. Spray from a passing car slapped against her face.

'Miss.' She turned. The driver had risen to his feet and was standing beside her, looking at her as if she were crazy. 'I cannot fix. The jack no work. Please, we sit in taxi and wait.'

Dorian shook her head. 'I can't wait,' she said. 'My plane will be leaving.' She peered ahead into the night. 'We're almost at the airport, aren't we?'

'Yes, but——'

'That's what I thought.' She reached inside the taxi and grabbed her holdall. The contents of the file she'd yet to look at—clippings, photos—all of it lay scattered on the floor. But it was too late now. 'I'll start walking,' Dorian said. 'If another taxi shows up, send the driver looking for me, will you?'

'Miss, please, you cannot.'

'Here.' She dug into her bag for some bills and tucked them into the bewildered driver's hand. 'Maybe I'll be lucky and someone will stop and give me a lift.'

'In New York?' The driver's voice carried after her as she began marching towards the distant airport. 'It will not happen, miss, and even if it should you cannot trust. Not in this city. Please. You must wait.'

But she couldn't, not if she was going to make that plane. Dorian's footsteps quickened. The driver was right, of course. No car would stop for her. This was New York, where only the fittest survived. You could fall to the pavement in the middle of Fifth Avenue and no one would acknowledge it. And he was right about the rest, too. In this city, you couldn't trust anyone, *especially* someone crazy enough to stop to pick up a stranger.

Not that that would stop her. You couldn't be a good reporter if you were afraid of——

A horn blared shrilly, making her jump. Dorian's head lifted sharply. Go on, she thought, have fun at my expense. A truck whizzed by, closer than it had a right to be to the verge; water splashed over her, cold as ice.

She shuddered and kept walking. How long would it take to walk a mile or two under these conditions? Twenty minutes? Half an hour? Would she make it on time, or——?

A car swept past her, swung sharply to the right, and came to a stop on the verge of the road just ahead. It was a sports car, something long and lean with a throbbing engine. Dorian blinked her eyes against the rain. Could it be...? Yes. Yes! The passenger door was swinging open.

She began running, her pace awkward in the muddy grass. When she reached the car, she paused and leaned down towards it.

The interior was dimly lit and leather-scented. Warmth drifted towards her, along with the faint strains of Tchaikovsky. There was a man at the wheel, but she couldn't see him very clearly. His face alternated between light and shadow from the headlights of oncoming cars. All she could tell was that he was tall and that his hands lay lightly—and powerfully—on the steering-wheel.

'Thank you so much for stopping,' she said, her voice a little breathless. 'You just saved my life.'

He turned slowly towards her, and for some reason her heart seemed to tighten in her breast. His face still alternated between light and shadow, but she could see that he had dark hair and eyes, a straight, handsome nose above what seemed to be a full mouth, and an arrogant tilt to his chin.

'Where are you going?' he asked. His voice was deep and soft, almost smoky. Dorian had the sudden crazy feeling that he never had to raise that voice at all, that people would do whatever they had to do to hear his words.

'You cannot trust,' the taxi driver had said. 'You cannot trust...'

Dorian touched the tip of her tongue to her lower lip. 'To—to the airport,' she said. 'But if you'd just be kind enough to take me as close to it as you can——'

'I'm going there myself. Toss your things in the back and get in.'

Dorian's heart did a funny turn again, as if someone had reached into her chest and given it a poke. It was silly, but the open door, the drift of leather-scented warmth emanating into the chill night from the car's interior, the smoky voice—all at once it seemed dangerous.

'Well?' The voice was amused now, even a little contemptuous. 'Are you going to stand out there and drown, or am I going to drive you to the airport?'

Dorian drew in her breath. What was there to fear? Men who drove expensive cars weren't likely to be serial killers, for heaven's sake. What she had to do was get to the airport and write the story of the year about a man named Jack Alexander, a man who might in hours become the absolute ruler of a country lost in the past.

'You're going to drive me to the airport,' she said briskly, and she tossed her bag into the rear of the car, climbed into the seat, and slammed the door after her.

CHAPTER TWO

DORIAN sighed thankfully as she sank into the leather bucket seat.

'It's a hell of a night for a stroll.'

She looked at the man who'd rescued her. He was smiling as he looked into his mirror and manoeuvred the car back into traffic.

She laughed pleasantly. 'Isn't it ever? I can't believe how hard the rain's coming down.' Her hair was dripping into her eyes; she put her hands to her face and shoved back the soaked strands. 'I'm afraid I'm going to make a mess of your car.'

The man beside her shrugged. 'Don't worry about it.' His foot settled more firmly on the accelerator. The engine growled as the car leaped ahead, the wiper clearing the windscreen in rhythmic strokes. 'What time does your flight leave?'

'What?'

'Your plane. I assume it must be taking off fairly soon or you wouldn't have risked life and limb on the road.'

'Oh.' She smiled. 'You sound like my taxi driver. He thought I was crazy to leave the cab.'

'That dead yellow beast on the verge was yours, then?' He nodded. 'I thought it must be.'

'Mmm. We had a flat—it was the final touch. Traffic was impossible all the way from Manhattan.' Dorian made an apologetic face as she looked down at herself. 'I really am making a mess of things,' she said. 'I didn't realise how soaked I was.'

Her rescuer glanced at her. 'You must be freezing,' he said.

She started to protest politely, but the sudden chatter of her teeth stopped her in mid-sentence.

'I suppose I am,' she said with a rueful little laugh. 'Who'd ever dream it would get chilly so late in May?'

'Well, we can warm things up a little.' He leaned forward and pushed a button on the dashboard. Warm air hissed from the heating vents and Dorian sighed with pleasure. 'Better?'

'Yes, thanks. Much.'

'There's a coat on the seat behind you. If you drape it over yourself, you'll be more comfortable.'

Dorian shook her head. 'No, thank you, that's all right. We'll be at the airport soon, and——'

'And by then you'll probably have pneumonia. Go on, get the coat.'

'Really, it isn't necessary. I'm feeling much warmer already. The heat's coming up, and——'

'For God's sake, woman, don't argue. Put the coat on.'

She stared at him. His voice had not risen; instead, it had taken on a note of command and she thought suddenly that he was a man accustomed not only to giving orders, but to having them obeyed instantly.

But not by her. It was one thing to accept a lift from a stranger and quite another to——

'You're soaked to the skin,' he said. She looked up. He was watching her, a little frown on his face. His gaze slipped over her, moving from her dripping hair to her damp face, then dropping to her wet khaki jacket. When his eyes met hers again, his face was expressionless. 'And you're cold, too.'

'I'm not. Really.'

A faint smile curved across his mouth. 'But you are,' he said softly, and suddenly she was painfully aware that her clothing must be clinging to her skin, outlining her breasts with intimate clarity.

Dorian felt her cheeks blaze. Be careful, she told herself. She'd been warned against crazies, hadn't she?

Her mouth tightened as she reached for the coat to hide herself from the man's coolly appraising gaze. He'd outmanoeuvred himself, though. Once she had the coat on, he wouldn't have much of a view to enjoy. She smiled as she snatched it up and draped it over herself from chin to toe.

'There.' His tone was light and pleasant. 'Isn't that better?'

'Perfect,' she said sweetly.

And it was. She was discreetly covered by the coat—his, she was certain, based on its size and its faintly masculine scent—and she was warm, as well...

And she'd done his bidding. He'd manipulated her into doing what he'd first commanded.

She blinked. Why on earth had she thought that? Besides, what counted was that she was warm again. The little tremors that had raced through her body had stopped. And it would have been stupid to have risked a chill at the start of her first big story...

'So.' He stretched lithely, shifting his weight in the bucket seat. 'You still haven't told me what's so urgent that you were willing to risk a night-time walk along the highway.'

'I did tell you.' Dorian's tone was politely neutral. 'I've a plane to catch.'

'Let me guess.' Her rescuer gave her a quick smile. 'You're off for a long weekend on the beach at Cancun.'

She laughed. Was that where people went for a weekend in his world? 'No,' she said, 'not hardly.'

'Martinique, then.'

'Not Martinique, either.'

He sighed. 'Ah, that's too bad. I was going to recommend a little place I know on the north side of the island—they serve the best rum punch this side of paradise.'

And he'd just love to take her there. Was that what came next? Dorian sighed inwardly. She knew all the moves by now, after five years of living in New York. You'd meet a man, there'd be a little chit-chat about dinner, or the newest nightspot, and then—as if the idea had just sprung into his head—he'd invite you to visit it with him. She'd passed up invitations to the Hamptons, to Miami, once even to Lake Tahoe for fun and games.

But Martinique? That was new to her list. Apparently the stakes were higher in this man's league. Still, why wouldn't they be? Everything about him spelled M-O-N-E-Y. Dorian stole a glance at him, her eyes taking in longish but expensively cut dark hair, the well-tailored suit, the Rolex Oyster glinting on his wrist. Yes, she thought a little disdainfully, he would know the best place on Martinique—and in half a dozen other pricey spots in the Caribbean.

She looked at the dashboard clock. Her mouth twisted. In a little while she'd meet Jack Alexander, and she had no doubt but that he would be much like the man seated beside her: wealthy, very sure of himself, good-looking— and never hesitant about turning on the charm for an attractive woman.

And yet—she stirred uneasily. And yet there was something else about the man driving this car, something she couldn't quite put her finger on. It had to do with the way he'd spoken to her, with the way he seemed to have forced her into a corner moments ago. It was as if a core of steel lay hidden just beneath the silken exterior.

She glanced at him again. There was something in the way he held himself, too, head high and shoulders straight, with just the slightest touch of arrogant pride to the set of his mouth. It was there in the way he drove this expensive car—a Porsche Carrera, she was fairly certain—with a skill and assertiveness that almost bordered on aggression, as if the caution of the slower-

moving drivers on the rain-slicked road was an insult to
his masculinity.

Her gaze fell on his hands, lying lightly on the steering-
wheel. They were tanned and well cared for, yet she was
quite certain they would be strong and powerful, that
they would not only be able to elicit the best from an
automobile, but from anything else they touched. From
a woman, she thought suddenly. A woman would re-
spond to him as the car was—with eagerness and
pleasure—and all at once she found herself wondering
what it would be like on Martinique, wondering if flowers
scented the air along the beach...

'...where you're going, if you want to make your plane
on time.'

Dorian turned towards him, afraid to breathe, afraid
she'd somehow spoken those last insane words aloud.
But she hadn't; he was watching the road, the car was
moving more slowly, and she realised that they'd turned
off the highway and on to the road that traversed the
airport.

'Excuse me? I—I didn't hear what you said.'

'I said, you'd better tell me where you want to be
dropped off, if you want to make your flight.'

Her brows rose a little. She'd been wrong, then. He'd
been gallant to the end; he'd given her a lift, flirted
probably no more than his male ego demanded, and now
he was all business. In fact, now that she looked at him,
she could see that he'd undergone a subtle change in the
last few minutes. That soft, sexy smile had been replaced by a certain grimness, and the hands that lay on
the steering-wheel gripped it almost tightly.

But then, he had a plane to catch, too. Dorian felt a
little twinge of something that surely couldn't have been
regret. She sat up straighter, took the coat from her lap,
and tossed it into the back seat.

'Of course. You can drop me off at—at...'

Where? Her breath caught. It was a damned good question, and she had no answer. She had no idea where to get the flight to Barovnia. Walt Hemple hadn't told her.

'Well?' Her rescuer slowed to a crawl. 'Look,' he said impatiently. 'I've a plane to catch myself and not a hell of a lot of time to do it in. Where shall I drop you?'

Her mind spun in frantic circles. What now? She glanced at the dashboard clock. Ten minutes? Ten minutes to make her flight. No, she thought grimly. Not her flight. Her career. If she missed that plane, she might as well never show her face at *WorldWeek* again.

'Come on, lady,' the stranger said. 'Where do you want to go?'

'I don't know,' she admitted.

His dark eyes narrowed. 'You don't know? What in hell is that supposed to mean?'

'It means—it means he didn't tell me,' she said a bit shakily.

His expression grew even more grim. 'He didn't tell you? You mean, you agreed to go away with some guy for the weekend without...?'

'No!' Dorian's eyes flashed with green fire. 'I certainly did not. And I resent the implication.'

His mouth seemed to soften a little. 'It wouldn't be so extraordinary, would it?' He smiled. 'A beautiful woman going away with her boyfriend for a couple of days, I mean.'

Some of the stiffness went out of her spine. 'No. I just—you had no right to assume——' She broke off. What in heaven's name did it matter *what* he assumed? He was a stranger; she would never see him again after this. She sighed and looked at him. 'I'm not going away for pleasure,' she said. 'I'm flying out on business.'

'Ah.' His smile tilted. 'As am I.'

'And it's—well, it's an important trip. But my boss forgot to tell me where my plane would be leaving from.'

His smile broadened. 'The problem's easily solved. Take a look at your ticket. The name of the airline will be on it.'

His suggestion gave her hope—until she remembered that all Walt had handed her was the library material and petty-cash voucher.

Dorian blew out her breath. 'I don't have a ticket.'

'I see. You're supposed to pick it up at the counter, hmm?' He shrugged before she could say anything. 'Well, call your boss and talk to him.' He reached for the cellular phone.

'No,' she said quickly, stilling his hand. He looked at her, brows lifted, and she gave him a nervous smile. 'You don't know him. I—I don't think he'd be very happy to find out that I'd screwed up.'

The stranger frowned. 'But it's his fault, surely.'

Dorian sighed. 'You don't know my boss. He might not see it that way.' Her shoulders rose and fell in a little shrug. 'This job I've been sent on is important, you see. It's hard to explain, but——'

'You don't have to explain.' He made a sound that was not quite a laugh. 'I know all about important jobs, and how they have to be dealt with even when they seem damned near impossible.'

Dorian nodded. 'Impossible,' she repeated—and all at once, to her horror, her eyes filled with tears. She blinked them back quickly, but not before he'd seen their tell-tale glitter.

'Hell!' His brows knotted together as he undid his seatbelt and moved towards her. 'No job is worth that.'

'This one is.' She swallowed hard. 'You don't under-stand——'

'I told you.' His voice was harsh. 'I *do* understand, better than you could possibly imagine.' His frown deepened, and then he began to smile. 'What if you just forgot about it?'

Dorian stared at him. 'What do you mean?'

'Your job.'

'Just—walk away from it?' She shook her head. 'I couldn't.'

'Why not? Where is it written that one must do whatever one is told?'

She gave a puzzled laugh. 'But that's what having a job is all about,' she said, watching him closely. 'You do what you have to do.'

He moved closer to her. 'What I said about Martinique is true, you know.' His eyes searched hers; he gave her a sudden, swift smile. 'We could have a late supper at that little place on the beach, then go for a walk in the moonlight.'

Dorian shook her head. So, she hadn't been wrong about his intentions after all. He'd been coming on to her all the time, just waiting for the right moment to make his move.

Still, she'd never had an invitation to any place as exotic as this. His line was different, she had to admit that—so different that it made her want to smile, something that had seemed impossible only seconds ago.

'I don't think so,' she said lightly.

He clasped her shoulders. 'Give me one good reason why.'

She smiled. 'Well,' she said, still in the same light tone of voice, 'it's pouring cats and dogs.'

He shook his head. 'Not in Martinique.' His hands moved slowly from her shoulders to her face. 'Believe me, I wouldn't dream of letting it rain in Martinique tonight.'

He looked deep into her eyes, and suddenly she wasn't smiling any more. No, she thought crazily, no, he wouldn't let it rain. He would make the moon come up, the stars fill the skies. He would—he would...

His gaze dropped to her mouth. 'Let me take you to Martinique, kitten.'

Dorian swallowed drily. 'Kitten?'

'That's what you looked like, standing there in the rain.' His gaze met hers. 'A little wet kitten, with its fur all matted down, needing somebody to dry it and cuddle it until it purred again.'

He cupped the back of her head; his hand gentled the silken strands of her hair that had dried in soft curls on the nape of her neck.

Dorian gave a little shudder. He was good at this, her brain said in a sharp whisper. He was very good. The way he was watching her, as if only she and he existed in the entire universe. The smile that promised pleasure. The soft, smoky voice that surely sounded as if he'd never said any of these things to another woman—it was all part of an act, one he'd probably used a dozen times before.

And yet—and yet...

'Sweet little kitten.' Her breath caught as he bent to her and pressed a light kiss to her damp hair. 'Say you'll come with me.'

Dorian shook her head. This was insane. It was—it was...

His mouth brushed her temple, then the curved arc of her cheek. 'Don't,' she said. At least, that was what she thought she said. But all she heard was the whisper of her own sigh as she lifted her face for his kiss.

Her heart pounded wildly as his lips met hers. Her hands crept to his chest, the palms flattening against his jacket.

'Say yes,' he whispered against her mouth, and all at once she wanted—she wanted...

A jet roared overhead, the sound filling the small, enclosed space like a peal of thunder. Dorian's eyes flew open. She stared at the stranger blankly, and then sanity returned. She pushed against him; he let go of her, and she scrambled back against the door.

'So much for gallantry,' she said. Her voice trembled.

For a long moment his face was expressionless. Then, finally, the corner of his mouth lifted in a cool smile.

'And so much for playing the reluctant maiden.' He turned away from her and shifted into gear. The car plunged off over the kerb and shot down the road. 'Have you figured out where you want to go yet, or are you still suffering from amnesia?'

Dorian's chin rose. 'You can drop me off at the International Arrivals building,' she said coldly. 'I'm sure I can get the information I need there—not that it matters now.'

His smile was like ice. 'Yes. You've probably missed your plane to Timbuktu or wherever it is you were going.'

'Barovnia,' she said, her tone curt. 'That's where I was going until you——' She cried out as the car came to a sudden halt. 'Are you crazy? I could have gone through the wind...'

'Barovnia? Did you say you're flying to Barovnia?'

'I said, I was *supposed* to fly to Barovnia.' She lifted her bag into her lap and folded her arms across it. 'But I won't be doing that now. *WorldWeek* will just have to get its news from pool reporters.' She swung towards him as he began to laugh. 'I suppose that seems very funny to you, that I'd be worried about missing a plane to a—a primitive little kingdom?'

His laughter stopped as abruptly as it had begun. 'If you think it's so primitive,' he said softly, 'why are you going there?'

Dorian stared straight ahead of her. 'Don't you mean, why *was* I going there?'

'All right. Why were you?'

All her anger came swelling up inside her. 'To report back to my editor on—on what it's like to watch a nation of poor peasants turn a man who's never done a useful day's work in his life into a little tin god.'

'Really.'

His voice was soft as the rain, as menacing as the night, but Dorian was too far gone to hear it.

'Yes, really. I know you can't understand why I'm upset. And I suppose, in a way, you're right. After all, nobody's really going to miss that report except me. I mean, what does the world give a damn about Barovnia? But I'm going to lose my...' She gasped and clutched at the dashboard as the car leaped forward. 'Dammit, must you drive like a lunatic?'

'I'm only trying to be helpful, Miss... What did you say your name was?'

'Oliver. Dorian Oliver. And it's too late to be helpful. While you were—while you were mauling me, my plane took off.'

The stranger flashed her a quick, cold smile. 'Relax, Miss Oliver. Your plane is still on the ground.' The tyres squealed as the car skidded to a stop. She watched, bewildered, as he got out of the car, came around to her side, and flung her door open. 'Do you have your Press pass, Miss Oliver?'

'Yes. Of course. But——' She caught her breath as he leaned into the car, caught hold of her arm, and tugged her unceremoniously out into the darkness. 'Would you mind explaining exactly what you're doing?'

He clasped her arm tightly as he marched her forward towards a building marked 'North Passenger Terminal'.

'I'm saving your job for you,' he said grimly.

He pushed the door open and tugged her into the lighted interior, and then he paused. There was a cluster of men near by, large men, all of whom had, apparently, been watching the door—and waiting, Dorian saw with some surprise, for their entrance. The stranger turned to her. 'Wait here,' he said in that same commanding voice he'd used to her before.

Dorian wanted to tell him what he could do with the order, but there was no time. He stepped forward and said something to one of the men, and then he turned to her again.

'This gentleman will escort you to the plane, Miss Oliver.'

'The plane?' Dorian stared at him. 'What plane?'

The stranger's lips drew back from his teeth. 'The plane to that primitive little kingdom. There's no other plane that could possibly interest you, is there?'

She knew what he was thinking, and she met his cold smile with a contemptuous stare. Had he really ever believed she'd given a moment's thought to all that nonsense about Martinique?

'None. But how did you ...?' Dorian put her hand to her mouth. Lord. Oh, lord. That air of authority. The wealth. The dark good looks. Was it possible? Had she spent the past half-hour with Jack Alexander—and had she, then, blown any slim chance she might have had of getting an interview with the man?

She ran her tongue over lips that had gone dry. 'Are you,' she whispered, 'I mean, it occurs to me that you— could you possibly be ...?'

He let her stammer and then, mercifully, he saved her from further embarrassment.

'Let me help you, Miss Oliver.' His voice was silken. He stepped closer to her, until he was only a whisper away. 'Will I be the new *abdhan*? That's what you want to know, isn't it?'

Dorian swallowed hard and nodded. 'Yes.'

He watched her for a long, long moment, his handsome face devoid of all expression, and then he gave her a smile that was colder than the rain.

'How could I be? The king of a primitive little country would have to be a barbarian, would he not?' He caught hold of her wrist; she felt the sudden, fierce pressure of his fingers on the fragile bones. 'He'd have to be a complete savage. Isn't that right, Miss Oliver?'

'Please.' Dorian grimaced. 'You're hurting me ...'

He almost flung her from him. 'Relax, Miss Oliver. I can assure you, I am not the *abdhan*.'

She watched as he turned and strode away from her. The cluster of men who'd waited politely throughout the interchange fell into step around him. Within seconds, they'd vanished into the depths of the terminal.

'Miss?' She turned, startled. The man who was to guide her to the plane had come up beside her. He was as soft-spoken as he was huge. 'We must hurry.'

Dorian nodded. 'All right. Just one thing. That man—who is he?'

Her escort took her bag from her as they began walking. 'Didn't he tell you?'

She shook her head. 'Is he a friend of the new *abdhan*?'

The man frowned. 'There is no new *abdhan*, miss. There is the anointed one, and there is the *abdhazim*—the Crown Prince, the next in line for the throne.'

'Well, that's what I meant. The *abdhazim*. Is he—was that man a friend of his? Is he part of the delegation?'

Her escort smiled for the first time. 'Yes. You may say that. He is part of the delegation.'

She had expected the answer. Still, it made her feel sick to her stomach to have it confirmed.

Her rescuer was a friend of Jack Alexander's, the man who never let reporters get near him. He was the *abdhazim*'s friend, and she had made an enemy of him.

Good work, she told herself with a sigh. Oh, yes, good work.

Dorian Oliver, girl reporter, was off to one hell of a great start!

CHAPTER THREE

STUPID, Dorian thought as her burly escort led her through the terminal, stupid, stupid, stupid! Her first shot at success, and what had she done? She'd damned near obliterated it—and that without having even left the United States! Given enough time, who knew what wonders she might manage?

'This way, please, miss.'

Her escort's hand pressed gently into the small of her back. He was hurrying her towards the boarding area.

Well, she thought grimly, at least he wasn't marching her out to the car park. For one awful moment, that had seemed a real possibility. Still, she wasn't on the plane yet. There was still plenty of time for things to change.

The man who'd picked her up on the road had probably reached Jack Alexander's side by now; he was probably telling him that Dorian Oliver of *WorldWeek* had already made up her mind about Barovnia and about him.

The things she'd said flashed through her mind like poisonous darts. She'd called the kingdom primitive, its people peasants, and Alexander himself—Dorian winced. Had she really called him a little tin god?

And if her words were being repeated to Alexander, who knew what might happen next? It was no secret that the next *abdhan* of Barovnia had no great love for reporters, not when it came to his private life. For all she knew, he was at this very minute listening to her rescuer's story, his face darkening with displeasure as he heard himself, and his people, described in such ugly terms.

'What's this fool's name?' he would demand, and the stranger would tell him.

'Oliver,' he'd say, 'Dorian Oliver,' and a big, silent man who might easily be the twin of the one at her side right now would be dispatched to wait for her, to bar her admittance to the Press section of the plane.

'You are not welcome on board this flight,' he would say, and how would she explain any of it to Walt Hemple, or even to herself? She was a reporter, for God's sake, she was supposed to exercise discretion, to say the right thing at the right moment and not run off at the mouth, especially to someone she'd never laid eyes on before...

'The steward will seat you, miss.'

Dorian started. They had reached the boarding stairs; her escort was smiling politely as he stepped away from her.

'Have a pleasant trip, Miss Oliver,' he said.

She nodded. 'Yes. Yes, thanks very much.'

The steward greeted her pleasantly. 'Your Press pass, please,' he said, and she handed it over, still half expecting a hand to fall on her shoulder.

But none did. The steward gave her an empty, mechanical smile, handed back the pass, and suggested that she might find a vacant seat back in the last few rows.

Dorian nodded. 'Thanks,' she said, and she set off down the narrow aisle, making her way carefully over outstretched feet and overstuffed shoulder bags that had pushed their way out from beneath the seats under which they'd been stored, saying hello to the few reporters she knew, trying not to gape at the famous faces interspersed in the crowd.

'Hey, Oliver,' a voice called out. 'Here's a seat, lover, you can sit on my lap.'

Dorian looked at the man from the *Mirror*. 'No, thanks,' she said sweetly, without missing a beat, 'I'd just as soon not share it with your belly,' and everybody chuckled.

'Oliver. Hey, Oliver. How come they hold the plane for good-lookin' broads?'

'Because bald guys aren't "in" this year,' she said airily, and there was more good-natured laughter all around.

Her sense of elation had returned by the time she settled into a seat. It felt wonderful to be among these people, to be on assignment along with the best her profession had to offer. As for the bantering, Dorian had grown used to it a long time ago, and she understood it, too.

Journalists—except for fools like her editor—didn't care if you looked like Quasimodo or Marilyn Monroe, so long as you got the job done. But journalism had always been a male-dominated profession. And, because of that, there were still certain rites of passage you had to endure before being accepted into its ranks.

Learning to trade one-liners, for instance. The newer you were, the more you had to prove you could smile and deliver as good as you got. Dorian had honed her skills on her very first job, back in Buffalo, New York, and she was still pretty good—on her better days, anyway.

She sighed as she tucked her bag beneath the seat. But this hadn't been one of her better days. First Walt Hemple, that ass, had all but asked her to seduce Jack Alexander so that she could get *WorldWeek* an exclusive. And then the man in the sports car had come on to her with a line so polished that it had—that she had...

There was no point in trying to pretend she hadn't responded to him. She had, even if it had only been for a second. Well, that was easily explained. She'd been worried sick about missing her flight—and he'd been an expert seducer. 'Let me take you to Martinique' indeed!

She blew out her breath and turned her face to the window. Lord, what nonsense.

'Oliver. Hey, Oliver! Why didn't you strip down before you took that shower?'

Dorian smiled and shot back an appropriate answer, and then she turned to the window again. The rain really was heavy, falling as steadily as when she'd first climbed into the stranger's car. Her gaze drifted up to the black sky, to where the landing lights of an approaching plane burned a path into the darkness, and suddenly his voice was in her head, soft and smoky and filled with promise.

'We could go for a walk in the moonlight.'

That was what he'd said. But it was such a corny line. Such a...

Was it raining in Martinique, or was the moon painting a beach with its silvery light? What would have happened if she'd said, yes, take me there, take me with you...?

'Good evening, ladies and gentlemen. On behalf of the Barovnian delegation and the crew of Global Airlines, we welcome you aboard. The captain has asked that you extinguish all cigarettes and...'

Dorian sat up straight and clasped her hands together in her lap. Thank goodness. The plane was moving, heading towards the runway. It was time to get to work. She had a job to do, and—come hell or high water— she was going to do it well.

The flight seemed endless. Dorian picked at her dinner, passed on the game of pinochle that started across the aisle, and tried not to let the snoring of the man beside her drive her crazy.

What time was it, anyway? She had no idea. Her watch had stopped working, courtesy, no doubt, of its exposure to rain, and the steward had done a vanishing act. All she knew was that she'd been crammed into this narrow space long enough for her toes to have pins and

needles in them, for the card game to have ended, and
for silence to have finally descended like a curtain over
the Press section.

But she was surprised when the seatbelt sign blinked
on and she felt the plane tilt gently earthward. It was a
nine-hour flight to Barovnia. Surely, they hadn't been
in the air that long?

The steward materialised out of nowhere, hurrying
quickly up the aisle. Dorian leaned across the mo-
tionless hulk of the reporter asleep beside her and caught
hold of the man's sleeve.

'Excuse me,' she whispered. 'Are we in Barovnia
already?'

He shook his head. 'No, miss, we're not.'

'But it feels as if we're coming in for a landing.'

'Yes. Mechanical troubles. Nothing to be alarmed
about, though, I assure you. We'll fix things up
and——'

'But where are we?'

Was it her imagination, or did he hesitate? 'Somewhere in Yugoslavia, I believe.'

'You believe? Don't you know?'

'I really can't say any more, miss.' He gestured towards the curtain that walled off the Barovnian delegation from the Press section. 'Security, you know.'

Dorian sighed. 'Once we've landed, can we at least
get out and stretch our legs?'

'Sorry. All passengers will have to stay on board.'

No, Dorian thought a little while later, not all passengers. It was the Press that had to keep to their
cramped quarters while the plane was on the ground.
The steward opened the front cabin door so that a fresh
breeze drifted in, but the Barovnians—the bigwigs,
Dorian's seatmate called them when the gentle
touchdown roused him from his sleep—were free to get
out and move about. She could see them through the
smudged windows, a little knot of men in dark business

suits standing incongruously in the middle of nowhere, caught up in animated conversation witnessed only by the grey dawn and an airport hangar that had clearly seen better days.

Dorian frowned. What kind of place was this, anyway? The runway was all but deserted, save for a couple of small, light planes that stood off to the side, and it was badly in need of patching.

Whatever mechanical problems had brought them down must have been significant, otherwise why would the pilot have landed at such a desolate spot? And yet— her frown deepened. And yet, no mechanic had so much as come near them. Not even the pilot had emerged to take a look at his craft.

There was no one on the apron at all, except for that cluster of men in dark suits.

All Dorian's instincts went on alert. Something was up, she was certain of it, and, whatever it was, the Barovnians were doing their damnedest to keep it from the planeful of reporters.

Dorian unbuckled her belt. The steward would have some answers, and, by heaven, if she couldn't get them from him, she'd—she'd——

Suddenly, a man stepped from the shadow cast by the plane; he'd apparently just emerged from the cabin. He said nothing, did nothing, but at the sight of him the little knot of conferees fell silent, seemingly commanded by his presence.

Dorian's brows rose. Well, she thought wryly, he was, indeed, an impressive sight. For one thing, he was dressed differently from the others. No dark business suit for him. He wore, instead, a white open-necked embroidered shirt of some silky-looking material, close-fitting black trousers, and knee-high black leather boots. An ancient leather jacket hung casually from his shoulder.

And he wore it all very well. He was tall and lean, with shoulders powerful enough to strain the seams of the shirt. He looked—he looked...

His face was in shadow, yet something about him reminded her of the man who'd rescued her from her broken-down taxi back in New York. No. It wasn't possible. Her rescuer had been the epitome of sophisticated urbanity, but this man—this man was...

Dorian caught her bottom lip between her teeth. Masculine. Fierce. Sexy. He was all of that, but the only other word she could think of to describe him seemed far more accurate.

He was dangerous. A funny tingle danced along her spine; she thought, suddenly, of a story she'd done on a new exhibit at the Bronx Zoo—and of the magnificent black leopard that had been its centrepiece, a creature lithe and splendid in its beauty, yet frightening to look upon because there was no mistaking the tautly controlled power contained within its hard-muscled body.

Dorian went very still. The man was stepping forward, moving out of the plane's shadow. Her heart slammed against her ribs.

He, and the man who'd driven her to the airport, were one.

She watched as the Dark Suits moved towards him. One of them spoke and the others nodded; there was a lot of gesturing, a lot of talking, and then he held up his hand, and they fell silent.

Dorian swung towards her seatmate, who had already laid back his head and closed his eyes, and jabbed him in the shoulder.

'Who is that?' she whispered.

'I'm too tired for guessing-games, Oliver.'

'Come on, take a look. Who's that out there?'

He groaned as he hunched forward and peered past her. 'The Barovnian Ambassador.'

Her heart sank. Dear lord, the man she'd insulted was the Ambassador. Well, she wasn't really surprised. She had seen the deference in the other men's behaviour. He had to be someone important——

'Or do you mean the other guy, the chargé d'affaires? Or the chief legate to the UN? They're all out there, Oliver, even a couple of Alexander's American advisers,' her seatmate said grumpily. 'Which man are you talking about?'

'That one,' she said, twisting towards the window again. 'The one wearing the riding boo...' He was gone, vanished as if by magic. 'He's gone,' Dorian said slowly.

The reporter beside her sighed. 'Goodnight, Oliver. Wake me when we touch down in Barovnia.'

'One last favour. Just tell me which man is Jack Alexander?'

Her seatmate yawned loudly. 'You don't really expect to find Alexander standing around out there?' He yawned again and settled back in his seat. 'Old Jaacov is tucked away in a private compartment up front, sleeping the sleep of the angels. Which is what I intend to do, Oliver. If you wake me again, it'd better be for a damned good reason.'

There already was a damned good reason for staying awake, Dorian thought. Mechanical troubles, the steward had said, but there still wasn't a mechanic in sight— there was only that cluster of men, drawn tightly together, in what appeared to be deep conversation.

She stirred uneasily. Something was up, but whatever was happening, the reporters would be the last to know— unless they found out for themselves.

Her pulse thudded as she got to her feet. The cabin was in darkness, window shades pulled against the pale morning light. Everyone was asleep—at least, they seemed to be, and the steward was nowhere to be seen.

Still, she had to be careful.

She moved quietly, slipping towards the front of the cabin and the door that stood ajar. Her heels clinked lightly on the metal boarding stairs and she held her breath, waiting for someone to shout a warning. But the steward hadn't heard her, and neither had the Dark Suits. They were on the opposite side of the plane—she could see them if she leaned out a little—and they were too caught up in conversation to notice anything else.

Dorian peered to where the ghostly hangar loomed against the lightening sky. Its door stood open. The interior was dark. The only thing she could see was the glint of metal and—and a figure, a tall figure wearing an embroidered white shirt.

She looked around quickly. No one had noticed her yet. There was an open stretch of ground between the plane and the hangar, but if she moved quickly enough... There was a story here, she was sure of it, something that would give her the angle she needed, that would separate her first dispatch from everyone else's.

Besides, what was the absolute worst that could happen if she got caught? A dressing-down from someone in the Barovnian delegation? Hell, any reporter worth the name had lived through that and worse. You were supposed to go after stories aggressively, and if you stepped on toes while you did, well, that was just part of the game.

Still, her adrenalin was pumping as she slipped out from the shadow of the plane. The hangar suddenly seemed a million miles away; her breath was whistling in and out of her lungs by the time she reached it.

She stepped inside the door and flattened against the wall. Her eyes swept the cavernous space. Yes. There was a plane, a small, sleek jet. But the man she'd followed—he was nowhere to be seen.

The jet blocked her view of the rear of the hangar. He was probably back there somewhere. She'd just have to check.

Dorian swallowed. There was a sharply metallic taste in her mouth. It was fear, but there was nothing to be afraid of. After all, what could possibly——?

A sudden loud whine filled the hangar. She spun around, hand to her throat, and as she did the whining noise increased until it was a roar.

Dorian's eyes widened. The plane—*her* plane—was—oh, God, it was moving. It was moving! It was racing down the runway and——

A hand, hard as steel, fell on her shoulder, the fingers biting sharply into her flesh.

'What in hell are you doing here?' a harsh, angry voice demanded.

She swung around again and stared into the furious face of the man she'd been following.

'The—the plane,' she stammered. 'It's leaving!'

His mouth curved downwards. 'I asked you a question, Miss Oliver. What in God's name are you doing here?'

Dorian shook her head. 'Didn't you hear me? Our plane—it's taken off. It's left us behind.'

He laughed coldly. 'A brilliant assessment. I suppose these are the superb sorts of intellectual skills that make you the fine reporter you are.'

'Dammit, don't you understand?' She twisted away from his hand. 'The plane to Barovnia just took off.'

He looked at her for a long, silent moment, and then he nodded. 'Yes.' His tone was clipped. 'It did exactly that.'

'But—but how could it? How could that happen? Didn't they know that we——?'

'How did you get off that plane?'

'The same way you did. I simply——'

She cried out as he caught hold of her again. 'There's nothing simple about it, Miss Oliver. You were told to stay on board.'

'Let go of me. Do you hear me?'

'You were given orders.'

'I don't take "orders",' Dorian said sharply.

His mouth thinned. 'So it would seem.'

Dorian's heart was slowing as things began to fall into place. There'd been a mistake, that was apparent. The plane had taken off without them, and if her absence hadn't yet been noticed surely his would be. The plane would turn around and come back for them in just a few minutes.

'Pretty sloppy security,' she said smugly.

'Yes.' His voice was grim. 'My thoughts precisely.'

'I mean, if they didn't notice that *you* were missing——'

'Didn't anyone try to stop you from leaving, Miss Oliver?'

'It's going to make a terrific story, though. "Two left behind at..."' She cried out as his grasp tightened. 'You're hurting me!'

'Two? Is that all your report will say? Just, "two"?' He stepped closer to her and his voice became a purr. 'No names, Miss Oliver?'

'I don't know your name,' she said, gritting her teeth against the pressure of his hand. 'And even if I did——'

'Don't you?'

'I only know that you've been the perfect gentleman from the moment we met.' She forced a cold smile to her lips. 'Manhandling me in the car, manhandling me now——'

'You're lucky that's all I'm doing.' His face darkened. 'Just why the hell did you follow me?'

'I didn't follow you. Not exactly. I just knew something was going on.'

His hand fell away from her. 'Did you.'

His tone was flat, turning the question into a statement. Dorian felt a chill tiptoe up her spine. In the excitement, she'd almost forgotten why she'd come after him in the first place, her conviction that something was happening that no one was supposed to know about.

Now, the feeling returned. She'd been right; something was going on.

But what? And what part did this man have in it?

Her chin rose in defiance. 'Yes,' she said, bluffing, 'and you might as well give me the details.'

He gave a short, sharp laugh. 'An exclusive interview, is that it?'

'Why not?' Dorian looked outside. The sun had risen; the sky was a pale, cloudless blue. 'We've plenty of time. The plane's not in sight yet, and——'

He laughed again and put his hands on his hips. 'Isn't it?' he said, as if she'd made some clever joke.

She hesitated. There was something in the way he was watching her that made her feel uneasy.

'For a start, who are you, anyway?'

'I thought you already had all the facts, Miss Oliver.'

'I never said that.' She trotted after him as he turned and began walking further into the hangar. 'What I meant was that there was time for you to tell me——'

She gasped as he swung towards her and caught her by the wrist.

'Exactly what do you know?'

'What do I...?'

'I've not time for games,' he said brusquely. 'Answer the question, dammit. What do you know?'

Dorian swallowed. 'Well, well... I know that we didn't really have mechanical problems.'

'And?'

'And—and...'

She fell silent. He stared at her for a long moment, and then he laughed.

'I should have known it was a bluff.' He let go of her and turned away. 'The answer's no,' he called over his shoulder.

'No?' What did that mean?

He stopped alongside the plane and ran his hand lightly along the burnished silver fuselage. 'No, I will not give you an interview.'

'But we have time before the plane comes back for us,' she said when she reached him.

He stepped to the wing and peered upwards. 'They won't.'

'Who won't?' Dorian ducked beneath the wing and scrambled after him. 'For goodness' sake, Mr—Mr whatever your name is, can't you speak in whole sentences? Who won't do what?'

He took his time, patting the silver skin as if the plane were a live creature, and then, at last, he turned to her.

'My name,' he said coldly, 'is Prince. Jake Prince.' He folded his arms across his chest. 'And what they won't do, Miss Oliver, is turn that plane around and come back for us.'

Dorian laughed. 'Oh, but they must. They can't just——'

'They can and will.' His voice was grim. 'The plane will go straight on to Barovnia.' He glanced at the little jet. 'And so will I.'

'In that, you mean? But I don't understand.'

'Then let me clarify things,' he said, his eyes never leaving her face. 'And let me do it in whole sentences, just so we're both certain you get the message.'

Dorian's cheeks reddened. 'I didn't mean——'

'Your colleagues—the ones who had brains enough to stay on board that plane—will land in Barovnia in a couple of hours.' He stepped beneath the jet, bent down, and removed the locking pins from the landing gear. 'It may take me a little longer,' he said, frowning as he walked slowly around the plane and scanned it, 'but I'll be there in plenty of time for a late breakfast.'

She stared at him. 'But—but what about me?'

He turned and looked at her. 'What about you?'

'You're not...' She took a deep breath. 'You're not thinking of leaving me here. You wouldn't do that, would you?'

'Wouldn't I?' He gave her a quick, wolfish smile. 'Have I mentioned that I'm of Barovnian ancestry, Miss Oliver?'

'No, you haven't. But what's that got to do with——?'

'I was born in that "primitive little country" you hold in so much contempt.'

Dorian paled. 'Look, just because I said some things——'

'Which makes me a barbarian. Wasn't that what we agreed?'

'No.' She shook her head. 'No, we didn't. It was you who said that. I never——'

'Reporters,' he said, his mouth twisting as if the word were bitter on his tongue. 'You're all alike—you think you can stick your noses in where they don't belong and never pay the consequences.'

Dorian drew in her breath. 'Look,' she began, 'I'm only doing my job. Your people invited the Press to come along on this junket. If you wanted to keep things from us, you——'

'And there's another thing. I did not manhandle you.'

'Mr Prince——'

'Not that I didn't come damned close.'

'What's that supposed to mean?'

He moved quickly, like the panther of which he'd reminded her. He was next to her before she could react, his hands on her shoulders as he drew her to him. '*This* is what I did,' he said, and his mouth dropped to hers in a quick, almost savage kiss. It lasted only an instant, and then he stepped back and gave her another of those cold, terrible smiles. 'Now,' he said softly, 'do we understand each other?'

'You're despicable,' she whispered. 'You're—you're...'

He laughed when she sputtered to silence.

'Don't tell me you've run out of adjectives, kitten. Where's the journalistic skill you're so proud of?'

Her eyes flashed with indignation. 'Don't you dare call me that again, dammit!'

'If you don't want to rot in this God-forsaken place,' he said briskly, as he turned away, 'you'd better get a move on. I want to be airborne in five minutes.'

'You're the most—the most horrible...' She caught her breath. *You'd better get a move on.* She touched the tip of her tongue to her lips. 'You'll—you'll take me with you?'

He turned, his hands on his hips. 'Tell me how to avoid it,' he said unpleasantly, 'and I'll be happy to oblige.'

Dorian nodded, trying not to let herself look as surprised—and relieved—as she felt.

'You're quite right. Deserting me here would only be bad publicity for——'

She gasped as he caught hold of her wrist. 'Just remember something. This is no cushy chartered flight.'

'Let go of me, please.'

'And I am not a steward, or one of your fellow reporters.' His eyes swept across her face. 'It would be a waste of time to try using that pretty face to get what you want, Miss Oliver. I'm not about to fall for the same nonsense you use on everybody else.'

'I get the message,' she said stiffly. 'Now, if you'd let go——'

'Just remember something. Once you set foot in that plane, you're nothing but an unwelcome passenger.'

Dorian stared at him, enraged. What a cold, unforgiving bastard he was. But what choice did she have?

'As I said before, Mr Prince,' she said finally, 'you're a true gentleman.'

He stared into her eyes while the seconds ticked away, and then he let go of her.

'Let's get started, then.'

He turned towards the boarding stairs. Dorian made a face at his retreating back as she massaged her aching wrist.

There were certain irrefutable truths about Jake Prince. He had lots of money. He could, when the occasion demanded it, turn on the charm. And he was, without question, the best-looking man she'd ever met.

But none of that was enough to make up for the fact that he was, first and foremost, an insolent, egotistical son of a bitch—and she could hardly wait for the moment she could shove that fact directly under his handsome, arrogant nose.

CHAPTER FOUR

SUNRISE was different when you saw it from the cockpit of a jet streaking across the sky. Dorian had seen the rising sun paint the towers of Manhattan in pale gold; she'd watched it blaze across the wheaten plains of her native Minnesota. But nothing had prepared her for the transfiguring glory of morning viewed from this lofty height.

The sun was a fierce golden ball, burning away the last remnants of the night. Below, mountain peaks burst into flames that spilled down into the valleys and banished darkness.

Dorian sighed. It was a breathtaking way to greet the day. It was just too bad that she had to share it seated beside Jake Prince—however, considering the circumstances, she supposed she had to be grateful she was sitting here at all.

He had not said a word to her since they'd left the ground, but then, he didn't have to. The set of his jaw, the stiffness of his spine spoke volumes. He resented her presence, and he had no intention of pretending otherwise.

She thought of those last moments in the hangar and how it had seemed he might leave her behind.

It hadn't been such an unreasonable fear. The truth was, she had no way of knowing what this man would do. He was not only a stranger, he was an absolute enigma, the more so as time passed. Each time she thought she had him figured out, he changed—almost before her very eyes—into someone else.

Who was Jake Prince, really?

Initially, Dorian would have had no difficulty describing him. He was a man used to money. The car, the clothes, the pricey watch were clearly all second nature. He had a smooth, sexy line and dark good looks that had to be appealing to many women. He was a man who had been handed all of life's goodies on a silver platter.

But there was, it seemed, quite another side to him. He was a man of influence and power in the Barovnian delegation. What she'd witnessed on the runway was proof enough of that. As for that easy charm he'd used on her when they'd first met—it gave way quickly enough to a steely determination.

He was not a man to be crossed, she thought, remembering again those moments in his car and the hangar.

She gave him a quick glance from under the dark sweep of her lashes. What was the great secret he'd been afraid she might know? What was he doing, making this very private flight to Barovnia? She had asked him about it the moment they were airborne, and his response had been direct, cold, and condescending.

'Don't waste your breath and my time, Miss Oliver. I've no intention of providing you or your magazine with bits of titillating gossip.'

Dorian's reply had been as swift as his. '*World Week* doesn't deal in gossip, Mr Prince,' she'd said. 'We're a news magazine. We provide information to our readers. If you'd ever bothered reading an issue, you'd know that.'

'Your publication is like every other glossy scandal sheet, Miss Oliver. It's not interested in fact.' His lips curled with distaste. 'You start out with preconceived notions, and you look around until you find something to support them. Then you print some trivia you label significant—and God knows how many fools rush out to plunk down their money just to be misinformed.'

'Has it ever occurred to you,' Dorian demanded, 'that *you* might be the one who's misinformed? I'm a reporter,

Mr Prince, not a—a scandal columnist. And my magazine——'

'There's nothing to debate. I am not going to be
interviewed.'

Lord, the arrogance of the man! Dorian swung towards him. 'I hate to disappoint you, Mr Prince,' she
said with saccharine sweetness, 'but I'm not interested
in interviewing you, necessarily. I'm only interested in...'
Dorian frowned. 'Which reminds me—what's your relationship to Jaacov Alexandrei, anyway?'

'Perhaps you didn't understand me, Miss Oliver. I'm
not going to give you any information at all.'

'But that's—that's ridiculous! Surely you can tell me
what part you play in the delegation. Are you one of
his American advisers? Are you an old friend? Are you
some sort of Barovnian representative?'

Prince ignored her questions. 'As for this little trip of
ours,' he said coldly, 'I wouldn't waste time planning on
ways to work it into your dispatches to your magazine.'

'And what, exactly, is that supposed to mean?' she
demanded.

'It means that this flight—and my part in it—are, for
the moment, not for publication for *WorldWeek's* eager
readers.'

'You can't be serious.'

'I've never been more serious in my life. This flight
is strictly off the record.'

'This may come as a surprise to you,' she said through
her teeth, 'but there are laws about a free Press.'

'In the United States, yes. But—in case you haven't
noticed—you're not in the United States any more.' He'd
looked directly at her then, his face a hostile mask. 'I
suggest you spend the rest of the flight thinking about
what that means.'

And Dorian had done just that as the plane droned
through the sky. Could he really keep her from filing
whatever story she chose? At first, she assured herself

that he could not. Barovnia might be still languishing in the Middle Ages, but she was an American citizen and a member of the Press, at that. She'd write what she damned well wanted.

But could she file it? She shifted uneasily in her seat. She had no idea what kinds of facilities she'd find in Barovnia, but if the Press's access to telephones and telegraphs was controlled or limited by the government it might be impossible to send stuff back to New York without interference.

What was so hush-hush about this flight, anyway? Dorian glanced at the man seated beside her. Why was Jake Prince at the controls of this little jet instead of in the cabin of the Barovnian charter?

She blew out her breath. And yet those weren't the million-dollar questions. The big one—the one that really needed answering—was the one that was at the heart of everything that had happened in the past hour.

What part did Jake Prince play in this story?

Dorian had come up with some theories, but each had holes.

Was he a Barovnian diplomat?

It hardly seemed likely. No diplomat would behave with as little tact as this man.

He might be one of Alexander's American advisers. But what American adviser would be powerful enough to say that he'd be the one to decide what a member of the Press could write?

And he really didn't seem terribly American. There was something about him, an air of masculine insolence he wore like a badge of honour, that suggested he hadn't come of age on the same side of the Atlantic as she had.

Dorian frowned. Jake Prince was an enigma. What sort of man could command a clutch of diplomats with a look? Or climb aboard a sleek, fast-moving plane and handle it with the same nonchalant ease he'd handled his sports car? Whatever he was, he was certainly not simply the rich, handsome playboy she'd written him off as at first.

Dorian's heartbeat stuttered. Prince. Jake Prince...

No. No, he couldn't be. It was impossible. She couldn't have got so lucky.

'... belt secured?'

She looked up, startled. 'Did you—did you say something?'

He nodded. 'I asked if your belt was secured.'

Her brain was spinning. Prince, she thought, *Prince*...

'Dammit, lady, it's not a very difficult question. Is the belt closed?'

'Yes. Yes, it is.' She touched the tip of her tongue to her lips. There had to be a way to keep the conversation going. 'Uh, why do you ask?'

He gave a negligible shrug. 'Just a precaution.'

'Just a precaution,' she repeated foolishly. Later, she would remember that simple statement and wonder at her inability to pick up on the meaning hidden within it. But just now she was too busy concentrating on what fate might have dropped into her lap to pay attention to reality.

'There's nothing to worry about, Miss Oliver. Just sit back and relax.'

Silence filled the cockpit again. Think, Dorian told herself, think! Keep him talking. There's got to be something...

She cleared her throat. 'I—uh—I suppose flying a plane like this takes a lot of training?'

Prince nodded. 'Yes.'

'It—umm—it must take a lot of skill.'

'Some.'

'And—uh—experience.'

'Right.'

It was all she could do to keep from groaning. Yes. Some. Right. At this rate, it would take the entire flight before she got a whole sentence from him.

She cleared her throat again. 'Have you been flying long?' He glanced across at her and she smiled politely. 'I mean, did you take it up recently, or have you always done it?'

It was, she knew, an inane question and yet, to her amazement, it did the trick. Jake Prince gave her a genuine smile—and an entire sentence in response.

'What you're asking is, do I really know how to handle this aircraft. Is that the question, Miss Oliver?'

Dorian clasped her hands in her lap. 'Yes,' she said, smiling back at him. 'That's right.'

'Well, you can breathe easy. I've had more than a thousand hours in planes like this one.'

'Is that a lot?' she asked pleasantly. 'I don't know anything at all about flying.'

'It's enough.'

He fell silent again, and Dorian's brain began whirling. Keep him talking, she thought furiously. Don't let him stop now.

'Well, that's good to hear. I've always wondered why airlines don't give passengers information about their pilots. You know the sort of thing I mean.' She gave a little laugh. 'Name. Place of birth. Experience.'

'Would it make you feel better if I said I've been flying since I was eighteen?'

He was clever, she had to give him that. He'd managed to neatly evade the two questions that really mattered. Still, it was the first bit of personal information he'd given her.

'Have you?' She smiled. 'You've been flying for quite a while, then?'

He nodded and shifted his long legs under the console. 'Almost twenty years.'

Her smile expanded. Another bit of information. Jake Prince was almost thirty-eight. How old, she wondered, was Jaacov Alexandrei? If only she hadn't left all that stuff from the research file on the floor of the taxi...

'Well,' she said brightly, 'that's interesting.'

His head swivelled towards her. 'Is it?'

'Oh, yes, absolutely. I never—I mean, it's so unusual to meet someone who knows how to fly...' Why was he watching her with such sudden intensity?

'Really?' He smiled politely.

'Really.' She hesitated. 'So, what else do you do? Besides fly, I mean.'

He leaned towards the console. 'I work,' he said, tapping his knuckle lightly against a gauge.

'At what?' His head came up, and she swallowed drily. Careful, she thought, careful, careful... 'I mean, I've never met anyone who—who knew how to fly before. I just wondered if you'd learned as part of—part of your job, or—or...' Why was he looking at her that way? Dorian's tongue felt as if it were tangling in her mouth. 'Or in the air force, perhaps,' she said desperately. 'Lots of young men learn to fly in the air force.'

'No, I took private lessons.'

If only she had her notepad, she thought furiously. Or her tape recorder. But both were tucked inside her bag, lying uselessly beneath her empty seat on the chartered jet. But it would be OK. She had a good memory. All she had to do now was find a way to get him to confirm her most important suspicion.

'In the good old USA.' He glanced over at her. 'That's the answer to your next question, isn't it?'

It took all her effort not to smile. Whoever Jake Prince was—even if he was the headline catch of a lifetime—he was, when you got right down to it, like every other human being in the world.

He loved to talk about himself and about his own interests. If she'd used her head and realised that from the start, she'd have——

'Unless, of course, you made the assumption that a country as primitive as Barovnia wouldn't have airplanes.'

Dorian looked up quickly. He was still smiling pleasantly, but an edge had crept into his tone.

'Why, no—no, I didn't make any assump——'

'Stop talking rubbish, Miss Oliver.'

She blinked. 'What?'

His smile fled, leaving his face cold and hard as granite. 'Do you think I'm a fool? All this charming chatter, the pretty smiles—I told you it wouldn't work on me.'

'But I wasn't——'

'Please, don't insult my intelligence.' He leaned towards the control panel again and tapped his finger against a dial. 'I know how you people operate.'

'You people?'

'I've dealt with reporters before. I know better than to trust them.'

'Mr Prince, I don't know what kinds of reporters you've known, but *WorldWeek* stands for honest reporting, and I——'

'Do you know what an oxymoron is, Miss Oliver? It's a figure of speech, using words that contradict each other.' He gave her a tight smile. 'Military intelligence, for example. Or holy war.'

Dorian's chin lifted. 'Look here, Mr Prince——'

'But my favourite is "honest reporting".' His smile grew even more grim. 'So before you toss out whatever lies you think will get you a scoop or an exclusive or whatever in hell it is you and your pals would sell your souls for——'

There was a bang, and a sudden, shrill whine filled the cabin. The plane began to shudder, and all at once Dorian's argument with Jake Prince didn't seem terribly vital.

'What's wrong?' she demanded.

Prince didn't answer, but then, Dorian thought wildly, how could he? He was flicking switches on the control panel with a swift precision that was, in itself, terrifying.

'Mr Prince? What is it?'

'We've lost an engine.'

'We've—we've lost an engine?' Her gaze fell to the sweep of mountains below, to their snow-capped peaks rising razor-sharp against the blue sky, and her heart seemed to stop beating. 'Are we going to crash?'

Prince shook his head. 'No. We can make it on one engine.' He hit another switch, and the plane steadied itself.

Dorian closed her eyes. 'Thank God,' she whispered. 'For a moment there, I thought——' Her words tumbled to a halt. The plane was losing altitude, heading slowly but steadily downwards. She swung towards him, her eyes wide. 'We're going down.'

He nodded. 'Yes.' His eyes never left the windscreen. 'Make sure that belt's tight, Miss Oliver.'

'But you said——'

'I know what I said.' His mouth narrowed into a grim line. 'This plane is designed so that it can fly on one engine—but, considering what lies ahead, I think prudence is the better part of valour.'

Dorian looked from Jake Prince's granite-like profile to the mountains ahead. Her hand went to her throat. They made the mountains that had preceded them seem insignificant, and she knew, without question, that he was right.

'I see.' Her voice shook a little. This was it, then. She was in a plane with a man she didn't know, in a place she'd never been, and they were about to crash.

'No.' His voice was clipped. 'You don't see. We're not going to crash.'

'You don't have to pretend,' she said quietly. 'Whatever's going to happen will happen.'

He reached across the narrow cockpit and put his hand over hers. Instinctively, she let her fingers curl into its comforting strength.

'There's a plateau ahead—do you see it?'

He jerked his chin towards the south and she followed the gesture.

'You mean, that little patch of grass?'

Prince nodded. 'We can set down there.'

'It doesn't look very large,' Dorian said softly.

His hand tightened on hers. 'Trust me, Dorian. I've landed in less space than that.' He gave her a quick smile. 'It'll just be a little bumpy.'

The ground was rushing up faster and faster. Dorian swallowed, then returned his smile as bravely as she could.

'Then I suppose it's a good thing we didn't have dinner service on this flight, isn't it? I'd hate to spill coffee all over my lap.'

He grinned. 'We'll have champagne on our next flight together, I promise.' He gave her hand one last squeeze, and then he clasped the control yoke. 'Just think positive thoughts,' he said, 'and before you know it we'll be down safe.'

Dorian nodded, but it was too late to think anything. The earth was coming up to meet them at an alarming speed. At the last minute, just before the wheels touched down, she closed her eyes tightly. There was a wrenching thud, a rushing noise, and then—and then silence.

'Dorian?'

She sat absolutely still, half afraid that if she opened her eyes she would see something awful.

'Dorian. Are you all right?'

She swallowed. 'I—I think so.'

She heard the clink of metal, the whisper of fabric, and then the touch of a hand on her face.

'Dorian. Look at me.'

Her eyes opened slowly. Jake was bending over her, his face dark. With anger, she thought—but then, suddenly, he blew out his breath and dropped to one knee beside her.

'You're all right,' he said.

She nodded. 'I think so. Yes. Yes, I'm fine.' She laughed shakily. 'Just a little scared.'

His hand stroked her cheek lightly. 'You've a right to be scared.'

She swallowed. 'Actually, it's more like terrified.'

He smiled, and she thought suddenly that it was a very nice smile, and that he had not smiled at her that way since—since just before he'd kissed her that first time at the airport.

'You should have trusted me,' he said. 'I told you I'd get us down in one piece.'

Dorian looked at him. Why should I have trusted you? she wanted to say. After all, you don't trust me.

But he was right not to trust her, wasn't he? Just before the engine had conked out she'd been playing games, trying to wheedle a story out of him while he—he had made her a promise and kept it.

Still, he hadn't been entirely truthful with her. She didn't know who he was. Although she had an idea. A damned good idea.

Her eyes lifted to his. 'Mr Prince?'

He smiled again. 'Yes?'

She touched her tongue to her lips; his gaze followed the gesture, then returned to hers.

'Considering the circumstances...' She paused. 'I—I—I have a question.'

'Yes,' he said softly, 'so do I.'

He bent and kissed her, his mouth warm and seeking against hers. She drew back in surprise and his arms went around her and gathered her close. Her lips parted. She told herself it was to whisper a protest, but when she felt the first brush of his tongue against hers a soft sound came unbidden from the back of her throat. Her hands came up; she leaned into him and caught hold of his shirt, clutching it tightly in her fingers, and the race of her heart and the pound of her blood obliterated all reality.

It was he who ended the kiss. 'Kitten,' he whispered.

Dorian's eyes opened slowly. He was holding her a breath from him; she knew that the flush of desire that crimsoned his cheekbones must be matched by her own.

It was hard to talk, at first. 'Jake.' She stared into his eyes. 'I didn't mean...'

He smiled. 'At least you've answered my question,' he said softly. 'I was going to ask if you didn't think it was time you called me Jake?'

Dorian hesitated. 'Is that—is that really your name?'

'What do you mean?'

'Well, it occurred to me that—that you just might be...' She swallowed. 'I was wondering if you might be the *abdhan* of Barovnia.'

Desire left his face. He looked at her coldly as he stepped back and rose to his feet.

'I suppose I should have expected that. A good reporter never stops thinking about her story, does she?'

'It's a logical question, Jake. You can't blame me for thinking——'

'Let me put your mind at ease, then. I am not the *abdhan*. And the only thing you'd better think about is that we've got to get out of here, and fast.'

She frowned. 'Shouldn't we wait with the plane? How else will the search party find us?'

Jake moved past her into the cabin. 'There won't be a search party.'

'Don't be silly. Once you put out an SOS——'

'I'm not going to draw my people in here, Dorian.'

'In where?' she said, staring at him. 'What in heaven's name are you talking about?'

'We've come down in the middle of the Askara Wilderness,' he said as he pulled open a locker and reached inside it.

'What does that mean?'

'It means,' he said grimly, 'that you're going to get the chance to take a long, hard look at a primitive territory inhabited by barbarians.'

Dorian got to her feet and put her hands on her hips. 'Very funny. But I've apologised for that remark too many times as it is. It's time you stopped trotting it out at every opportunity.'

'There's nothing even remotely funny about our situation.' He was stuffing things into the sack as he spoke. Two lap blankets. Chocolate bars. A couple of cans of Coke. 'This is a place where it's impossible to tell the good guys from the bad. So, unless you want to risk researching what it's like to be the night's entertainment, you'd better get your pretty butt in gear and follow me.'

Dorian blinked. 'You're joking.'

Jake looked at her. 'Do I look as if I'm joking?' he asked coldly.

No, she thought, he didn't. But he couldn't really be serious. A primitive territory? Bad guys you couldn't tell from good guys? Barbarians?

And all at once she understood. The engine malfunction had been real enough—instinct told her that Jake Prince wasn't the sort of man who'd fake something as dangerous as a landing on a plateau the size of a breadboard—but the rest was nonsense. He'd seen his chance to make her eat her words about primitive countries and barbarians, and he'd leaped at it. This was payback—an exhausting hike to Kadar, the capital of Barovnia, which was probably an hour or two away—and he'd have had the last laugh.

Well, he could just take his nasty little scheme and shove it.

Dorian smiled sweetly. 'Are you ready to leave?'

Jake nodded as he snugged the sack shut and hoisted it on his shoulder.

'Yes. The Cristou Mountains are just ahead, and——'

'Well, then, have a good trip.'

He straightened and stared at her. 'What?'

'I said, have a good trip. I'll stay here and wait.'

Jake's eyes went flat. 'For what? I've just told you——'

'I know what you told me.' She shrugged lazily. 'I'll take my chances with the—what do you call the people who inhabit this place?'

'Dorian. Listen to me.'

Her smile fled. 'No,' she said, shaking her head, '*you* listen for a change. I know what this is all about. I know what you're up to. You're determined to make me eat my words about—about—you know, the primitive country thing, and——'

'Do you really think I'm that petty?' he asked quietly.

For a second, her resolve faltered. But then she looked into his cold eyes, and her spine stiffened.

'I'm not budging. If you're going, you go alone.'

'Get up, Dorian.'

His voice was ominously soft. But she was tired of being intimidated by this man. It was time to put a stop to it.

'No. I'm not going with you.'

'Get up!'

She stared at him. He looked suddenly dangerous, and she thought again of the panther, but it was too late to back off.

'I'm not taking orders from you, Jake.'

He stepped closer. The look on his face made it difficult not to shrink back in defence, but she held her ground.

'I've no time to play games,' he said.

'Good. Then you'll stop all this foolishness, turn on the radio, and call for help. Or must I do it my——?'

She cried out as he bent towards her, but he didn't touch her. Instead, he reached for the microphone and ripped it from the console.

'Hey,' she said. Doubt crept into her voice. 'What'd you do that for?'

'Just in case you get any ideas. I told you, I don't want my people drawn into this place. Now.' He straightened and stared down at her. 'Are you coming with me or aren't you?'

Dorian gave a nervous laugh. 'Come on, Jake. Don't you think you're carrying this a little too far...?'

Her voice drifted to silence as he pushed open the door. 'Good luck,' he said, and then, to her absolute astonishment, he dropped lightly to the ground and trotted off across the silent meadow.

CHAPTER FIVE

OBVIOUSLY, Jake didn't know when it was time to admit he'd lost the game.

Dorian blew out a breath. It had taken a moment to figure out, but once she had it all fell into place. Jake had expected her to swallow his fanciful tale of bogeymen and danger, and when she hadn't he'd been caught short. That arrogant male pride of his had kept him from admitting that he'd invented the story, and so he'd marched off across the meadow without so much as a backward glance.

She shaded her eyes with her hands and watched his receding figure. The only question now was what would happen next. How long would he let her stew in her own juices before he came back to collect her? Because that was what he'd have to do. Despite all the dramatics with the radio, there would undoubtedly be a search party on the way, and he couldn't very well let it find her alone.

Dorian smiled. She could just imagine him trying to explain his way out of that situation.

'Jake Prince went off and left me here,' she would say bravely, first for her rescuers and then for the media. 'I suppose he thought he would be safe, leaving a defenceless woman alone in a—a wilderness. I guess he thought he would never be found out. I mean, he kept reminding me that no one knew I was on board the plane with him.'

She laughed softly as the dark forest swallowed him up. 'Sorry, Jake,' she murmured as she settled in to wait. 'I'm afraid you've underestimated me.'

She wondered again how long it would take him to come trudging back. He had, at best, only minutes to play with—and then, she thought smugly, he would have to admit defeat.

At first, she watched the forest, waiting for the first sign of Jake's return, but after a while that got dull and so she kicked off her shoes and sat down in the open doorway, gazing around the plateau instead, watching the grass and the few spring wild flowers that had already blossomed bend under the gentle whisper of the breeze.

But none of that made time move any more quickly. It seemed to have come to a standstill, and she told herself that it was only because her watch had stopped working. When you couldn't see the minutes change, they seemed to drag. She remembered a day last winter when the newsroom clock had gone on the blink and everybody had joked about not knowing whether they'd put in eight hours or eighteen without its pulsing digital face to read.

But it did seem as if Jake had been gone quite a while. How far would he push this nonsense, anyway? She began to think about what excuse he'd offer when he had to come back and face her, and gradually she decided that only one had any possibilities at all.

All right, he'd say in a brusque, no-nonsense voice, I misjudged where we came down. This isn't the Askara Wilderness at all. There's a road just beyond those trees and, surprise, surprise, Kadar is an easy couple of miles away and you won't mind just going for that brief stroll with me, will you, Dorian?

She smiled. 'Really, Jake,' she said into the silence.

Her voice seemed loud, almost unnatural, an alien presence intruding on the warm air, and she felt a faint stir of uneasiness. What a strange place this was, this deserted sea of grass. There wasn't any sign of life out there, not even a bird or an insect.

And the silence. It was so total. So complete. So—so penetrating.

Jake would probably tell her there was no such thing, that the phrase was—what had he called it? An oxymoron. But how else could you describe such quiet? It *was* penetrating. She could hear it drumming in her ears, feel the heaviness of it in each breath she took.

If only Jake would come back.

Dorian caught her bottom lip between her teeth. Just so she could tell him what she thought of him, of course. That was why she wanted to see him come striding across the meadow, so she could look him straight in the eye and say, Jake Prince, you damned fool, don't you think you've...?

What was that?

Her heart leaped like a frightened rabbit, lodging somewhere between her throat and her breasts. Something was out there. She'd heard it, a sound, a low sound, like—like...

'Jake?' she whispered.

She waited, pulse thudding, but there was only silence. That terrible, unnatural silence. It took all her courage to lean forward and peer cautiously out of the door. But there was nothing to see. Of course there wasn't. There was nothing out there but grass. The endless grass, stretching to the dark, dark trees.

Dorian wrapped her arms around herself.

'You're playing straight into his hands,' she muttered to herself. If she kept this up, she'd be a basket case by the time Jake returned, and that was what he wanted, wasn't it? He'd stalked off and left her here because she hadn't fallen for his silly stories; he had to be counting on her going to pieces while he was gone, then doing something ridiculous when he reappeared, something she would never be able to live down.

She blew out her breath. What she had to do was concentrate on something else. On—on what had happened so far. Jake had said she couldn't write about their flight, but who was he to give orders? This whole thing would make terrific copy. The mysterious flight. The forced landing. And Jake. Jake would make the best copy of all.

Did he really think she couldn't write about him just because he'd refused to give her any information about himself? A smug little smile curled across Dorian's mouth. She knew enough about the enigmatic Mr Prince to make *WorldWeek's* readers forget their morning coffee.

Jake Prince, the arrogant, opinionated mystery-man of the Barovnian delegation, spent the morning alone with this reporter. Although his relationship with Jack Alexander, the man who may well be the next Barovnian abdhan, *is not clear, it is obvious that he has the power to influence many of the policies the* abdhan *will . . .*

And he knew something. Something big. She was sure of that. He was hiding a secret, the kind that would make a name for the journalist who unearthed it, and she was determined to be the one who did.

Dorian frowned. It wouldn't be easy, though. Jake had said he'd tell her nothing, and he didn't strike her as the sort of man who ever went back on his word. He was harsh, he was hard. He was insolent and cold and totally unapproachable, but she couldn't imagine him saying something and not following through . . .

And he'd asked her to go away with him, a lifetime ago, before he'd known who she was or where she was going. What would have happened if she'd said yes? Would he have given up his role—whatever it was—in the delegation for a night with her? Would they have walked along the beach in the moonlight? Would he have taken her in his arms and kissed her and kissed her until they sank down into the sand, until . . . ?

Oh, God!

There it was again, that sound. Dorian felt the blood draining down to her toes. There was definitely someone out there, just as Jake had said. Why had she ever thought he'd made the whole thing up? He wasn't a man who played get-even games: if he were, she'd still be standing at the airport, trying to figure out how to tell her boss she'd been blackballed from the flight to Barovnia.

The sound came again, carried on the breeze, this time accompanied by a metallic clank, like a bell pealing mournfully in hell.

Dorian moaned, jammed her fist against her lips, and scooted deeper into the plane. Whoever was out there was coming closer. And that sound—that pitiful, keening sound, was enough to—to...

Her shoulders hit the wall, and she turned her face to it. 'Jake,' she whispered, 'Jake, please...'

There was a scrabbling sound at the door, and she swung towards it, her fists upraised in defence and terror in her heart...

It was Jake, Jake silhouetted in the doorway. She uttered a sob and flew to him, wrapping her arms tightly around his neck, savouring the comfort of his embrace as his arms closed around her.

'What is it?' he demanded. His voice hoarsened with concern. 'Are you hurt? What happened?'

She shook her head as she burrowed deeper into his arms. 'No,' she said, her voice shaky and muffled against his shoulder. 'I'm all right now.' She could hear the steady thud-thud of his heart, smell the sunlight and the meadow grasses in his scent, and she knew suddenly that she had never in her life felt this safe before.

He held her for a long moment, and then he clasped her shoulders, drew back, and looked into her face.

'I shouldn't have left you,' he said grimly. 'Hell. I knew it the minute I——'

'It was my fault,' she said breathlessly as she peered past him. 'I should have believed you. Oh, Jake, there's someone—there's someone...' She went stiff in his arms.

'Dorian? What...?'

A black and white cow stepped delicately out of the trees and into the meadow, mooing plaintively to the sound of the brass bell that hung from its neck.

Suddenly, all Dorian's pent-up rage came tumbling out. Her boss had humiliated her, Jake had humiliated her, and now this—this stupid beast had finished the job.

She drew a deep breath and wrenched free of him.

'You—you rat,' she spat. 'You worthless bastard. You—you...'

Jake's brows rose. 'I take it you're feeling better,' he said drily.

'The hell with you, Jake Prince.' She slammed her fist against his chest. 'Lying to me, making me think that—that there were things out there...'

He caught hold of her wrist before she could hit him again. 'There *are* things out there,' he said tightly.

'Cows,' she said, spitting out the word as if it were a curse. 'That's what's out there. Cows!'

Jake glanced over his shoulder. 'Yes.' There was no humour in his voice. 'That's right—which means we've more reason than ever to get out of here now.'

'Oh, please! I've milked far too many cows to run from one now, Jake. I hate to tell you this, but the party's over.'

A quick smile twisted across his mouth. 'Cows, Miss Oliver? At *WorldWeek* magazine?'

'At home, in Minnesota, not that it's any of your business.' She gritted her teeth as she twisted uselessly against his hand, then raised her reddened face to his. 'All right, you've had your fun. You filled me full of lies and I swallowed just enough of them to go to pieces over nothing. Are you satisfied?'

Jake's mouth curved downwards. 'I'll be satisfied when we've got the hell out of here,' he said. He glanced down at her feet. 'Go on, get your shoes on and let's get moving.'

'Uh-uh.' Dorian shook her head and crossed her arms over her breast.

'Uh-uh?' He went very still. 'What does that mean?'

'It means,' she said with great precision, 'that nothing's changed. I am not budging from this plane.'

He smiled. Although it was not really a smile, she thought suddenly. It was—it was just a drawing back of his lips, a quick flash of white teeth, and it sent a shiver down her spine.

'I could have been almost to the pass by now,' he said softly, so softly that she had to strain to hear him.

The pass? What pass? What was he talking about?

'. . . stupid enough to come back for you.'

Dorian tossed her head back. 'I see.' Her voice was sugary. 'You came back for me.'

Jake's eyes narrowed. 'Yes. But I'm beginning to wonder why I bothered.'

She smiled. 'Why, Jake. You came back because you're a gentleman. We both know that. Everything you've done, from the moment we met, has proved how gallant you are.'

A muscle knotted and unknotted in his jaw. 'Don't be clever, Dorian,' he said softly.

'Why *did* you come back?' She gave him a wide-eyed, innocent smile. 'Come on, I'm sure you can come up with something creative.'

'Maybe I don't want your blood on my hands.'

'That's it? You can't do better than a hackneyed old bit like that?'

'Dammit, woman! I've no time for games.' He took a step towards her and then, with a swiftness that stole her breath away, he gathered her to him and kissed her.

It was a kiss unlike any she'd ever experienced. There was no gentleness in it, no tenderness; there was, instead, a wild, fierce passion that should have been terrifying.

But it wasn't. She felt the raging heat of his body as he held her to him, felt the questing demand of his mouth on hers, and before her heart could manage a beat she was on fire.

'Yes,' he said against her mouth, and he drew her closer until there was nothing in the universe but him, nothing but the feel of his lips, the heat of his hands, the urgent need of his hard body.

She was trembling when the kiss was over, and unsure of which of them had ended it. Her eyes opened slowly and focused on his face, and she knew that it had been he who'd ended it.

That she'd responded to his passion was humiliating enough, but this knowledge—that he had been able to think, to stop what was happening even while she was drowning in a whirlpool of desire—was devastating. She took a deep breath, then laid her hands against Jake's chest.

'You can let go now,' she said. Her voice was steady despite the fact that inside she was a churning mass of warring emotions. 'You've made your point.'

A muscle ticked at the corner of his mouth. 'Have I?'

'You Tarzan, me Jane. That's the message, isn't it? Big, brave man comes back to save terrified woman.' She forced her eyes to meet his. 'I suppose you thought I'd fall into your arms with gratitude.'

He drew her close to him again and she could feel the evidence of his desire.

'You know what the message is, Dorian.' His voice fell to a husky whisper. 'I should have taken you in my car, back in New York.'

Stunned, she stared into his insolent, unsmiling face, and then she balled her hands into fists and pushed against his unyielding chest.

'You bastard! Who do you think you are? How dare you——?'

'I could have found a motel for a few hours, and you'd have come to me, all quicksilver passion and desire, and to hell with the rest of the world.' She began to struggle against him; his hand slid up to the column of her throat and he cupped her face and held it still. 'I could take you now, just as easily,' he said, his eyes fixed on hers, 'in this plane...'

'You... you son of a bitch. You—you——'

'Or outside, in the meadow, with the sun heating your skin and the grass beneath you.'

He bent to her and she struggled to turn her head, but he was strong, far stronger than she'd imagined. His mouth touched hers, gently, almost lazily, his kisses slow, druggingly sweet, and, to her horror, she felt the tremor start within her again, felt her bones turning to honey.

Images blazed behind her closed eyelids: Jake, beautiful in his nakedness, his shoulders blotting out the sun as he came down to her; Jake, touching her flesh with slow, intimate knowledge, putting his mouth and tongue to all her secret places...

Dorian groaned softly, and instantly a triumphant smile curved across his mouth.

'That's right, kitten. Think of how it's going to be when I finally take you.'

The smug words set her free.

'And that's exactly what you'd have to do to make love to me,' she said, her eyes meeting his. 'You'd have to take me, Jake, because I'd never go to you willingly.'

He laughed. 'Making love is just a fancy term for what we both want, Dorian.' Her hand shot up and he caught hold of her wrist, his fingers like steel on the fragile bones. 'Temper, temper,' he said softly.

She stared at him, her breasts rising and falling quickly, as if she'd just run a mile.

'I hate you,' she said in a low voice. 'Do you understand?'

His teeth glinted in a quick, cold smile. 'I'd love to continue this discussion, but I'm afraid we're running out of time.'

Dorian tossed her head. 'Don't tell me we're back to that!'

'Last chance,' he said. 'Either you come with me willingly, or——'

'Or?'

'If I have to drag you out of here, it won't be pleasant for either one of us.'

'I'll wait here, thank you.' She wrenched free of him and leaned against the bulkhead. 'The search party ought to be here soon, and——'

'Are you stupid?' He reached out and caught hold of her wrist. 'There won't be a search party. I told you that.'

'You told me lots of things, and they were all lies.'

Jake's mouth whitened. 'I am a lot of things, Miss Oliver,' he said softly. 'I am, perhaps, some of the things you've called me. But I am not—and never have been—a liar.'

She stared up into his cold, furious face, and, for the first time, real doubt crept into her mind. She knew little about Jake Prince and what she knew she didn't like—but would he lie? 'Do you think I'm that petty?' he'd once asked, and all at once she was fairly sure she knew the answer.

But if he wasn't lying, then his stories about bandits and barbarians were true. And if they were, then—then right now, this very minute...

'Yes,' he said, reading the growing fear in her eyes. 'That's right. We've pushed our luck as far as we can.

Any minute now it's going to start running out. Now, get your shoes on and let's get the hell out of here.'

He let go of her and turned towards the open doorway. Dorian stared after him while her brain worked furiously. Which was it? Was he telling her the truth? Were there men out there—cruel men, who got pleasure from rape and things that might even be worse? Or was it all a hoax? Was there nothing out there more harmful than a cow?

'Well?' Jake looked at her, his face dark. 'Which will it be? Do I throw you over my shoulder and carry you, or are we going to do it the easy way?'

Would he carry her, if she refused to go with him? Yes. He probably would. And if she was right—if there was a search party on the way, or if Kadar was a stone's throw from here, that was not quite the way she'd want to make her entrance, draped like a bag of laundry over Jake Prince's shoulder.

It didn't really matter if he was telling her the truth or not. The walk to Kadar would make terrific copy. That was reason enough to give in and go with him, wasn't it?

'All right.' Jake moved swiftly towards her. 'That's it. You've had your chance——'

'No,' she said quickly. 'I mean, I've—I've decided to go with you.'

His eyes fastened on hers. 'But you still don't believe me,' he said softly, 'do you?'

'Does it matter?'

The muscle moved in his jaw again. 'No.' His voice was chill. 'No, it does not. Just so long as you do as you're told, we'll get along just fine.'

Dorian shrugged her shoulders, then bent down to get her shoes. 'I'll do whatever makes sense,' she said.

When she straightened up again, she found Jake watching her, his hands on his hips.

'You've pushed and pushed,' he said softly. 'And now I'm warning you, Dorian. Don't push me any further.'

She flushed. 'I might give you the same message.'

'You're to stay right behind me,' he said, ignoring her remark, 'and you're not to say a word. Is that clear?'

'Yes, sir.'

Jake's mouth tightened. 'We're going to make straight for the trees. Once we're in the forest, try to put your feet exactly where I've put mine.'

Her mouth opened in the start of another quip, but she thought better of it.

'OK.'

He nodded. 'Let's go, then.' He took her hand and drew her towards the door, and then he stopped. 'One last thing. If anything happens to me, don't stop. Just keep heading for the trees. That way, you'll stand a chance of making it.'

The words, and the way he said them, stopped her short. 'Jake,' she breathed, 'Jake, wait a minute...'

He bent and kissed her, hard and fast, then drew back and gave her a quick smile.

'OK,' he said. 'Down the steps and let's hit the ground running.'

And, since he still had her by the wrist, that was what she did.

The trees were further away than she'd thought. She was panting by the time they reached them, and she put out a shaky hand.

'You've got to let me stop and catch my breath,' she gasped.

'Shut up,' Jake hissed.

She groaned as he tugged her after him until they were well within the dark forest. Branches whipped into her face and pulled at her hair like witches' claws. When he finally whispered that they could take a break, she sank back against a tree trunk and drew great gulps of air deep into her lungs.

'Better?' His voice was low.

'Yes,' she puffed, and then she was sorry she had answered because it made him take hold of her hand again and push her deeper into the woods.

This time, she didn't waste breath begging him to stop, she just kept going, stumbling on rubber legs. It was all beginning to seem brutally real. Jake's behaviour was more than cautious. He was—he was behaving as if the forest really might be dangerous.

They stopped suddenly, and his arm snaked around her and drew her tightly into the hard curve of his body.

'Stay perfectly still,' he hissed into her ear.

Dorian did more than that. She stiffened, her body becoming rigid. There were sounds in the brush. Voices. Voices. Men's voices, speaking in a strange language. There was a guttural savagery to the voices that—that...

She buried her face in Jake's shoulder and he held her close, his hand stroking her hair, until the voices faded away, and then he squeezed her hand.

'OK,' he whispered. 'Let's move.'

Each footstep sounded like a gunshot, each snapping tree branch like a whip. All she could pray now was that she'd been right, at least, about Kadar: that it was not terribly far, that reaching it would be an easy walk.

They came out of the forest suddenly, stepping with no warning from darkness into sunlight. Ahead lay an endless plain with a single, badly rutted dirt road angling across it.

Dorian blinked. 'But—but where is Kadar?' she asked in a breathy whisper.

It seemed to take forever until Jake answered. 'Do you see that mountain?'

She did. It rose like a tiger's tooth far in the distance.

'Yes,' she said. 'But—but you don't mean...' She swallowed. 'You can't mean...'

'I do mean.' For the first time, there was a quality that just might have been compassion in his voice. 'Those are the Cristou Mountains, Dorian.' He put his arm around her shoulders and drew her closer. 'And Kadar,' he said softly, 'is on the other side.'

CHAPTER SIX

DORIAN glanced up at the sun. It had been high overhead when they'd begun their trek; now, it was midway
towards the horizon. How long had they been at this,
anyway? A million hours, by the feel of things. She was
weary and sweaty, and the sole of her right foot felt as
if it were slowly turning into hamburger. Her thin, low-
heeled pumps had been designed for pavement, not for
narrow dirt roads.

Jake had set an unrelenting pace, one she'd had trouble
matching. But she'd been determined to do it, driven as
much by pride as by the cold chill that seemed to have
settled between her shoulder-blades, the feeling that
someone might just trot out of the forest and come after
them.

After a while, keeping up with him had become impossible. He had a long-legged, lean-hipped stride—it
took almost two of her steps to match one of his—and
finally she'd asked him if he could please slow down a
little. By then, she'd fallen in just behind him and he
hadn't even bothered looking back when he'd answered
her question with one of his own.

'Can't you keep up?'

She hadn't been able to see his face, but then, it hadn't
been necessary. His tone had oozed cold disdain.

So much for compassion, she'd thought grimly, and
she'd tossed back a quick response that had nothing at
all to do with the truth.

'Of course. I was just hoping I could have more time
to enjoy the scenery.'

That, she'd noted with satisfaction, had caught his attention. Jake had stopped dead in his tracks and swung around to face her.

'In case you hadn't noticed,' he'd said coldly, 'this is not a guided tour.'

'No,' Dorian had answered, trying not to let him see that she was breathing hard. 'But it will be part of the dispatch I file.'

'I told you, you aren't going to be filing a story about this.'

Her smile had been sweet enough to lure an ant colony into a trap.

'So you keep saying. But I will, eventually. You know that.'

'Really?'

His voice had become a threatening purr and she'd hesitated, suddenly wary of angering him in this desolate place. But then she'd looked into that hard, implacable face and her courage had come back in spades.

Who was Jake Prince to think he could give her orders?

'Really,' she'd said, very calmly and very quietly. 'Please don't forget that it's my job to tell *WorldWeek*'s readers about things that will interest them.'

Jake's eyes had gone dark. 'No,' he'd said in a chilly voice, 'I won't forget it, Dorian. Not for a minute.'

And then he'd turned abruptly and marched on, never so much as sparing a glance to see if she'd followed him or not.

Dorian made a face as a branch snagged her cotton jacket. As if she had a choice, she thought as she wrested it free. How else would she find her way to Kadar, if not trailing ten paces to the rear of Jake Prince? Her mouth turned down. Ten paces to the rear was how he preferred it, too. She was certain he was the kind of man who liked his women docile and valued them slightly less than his favourite polo ponies.

She wondered, once again, just how long she'd been trudging along in Jake's footsteps, following him mindlessly down this road like some—some servant girl out of another century. Yes. That was how she felt—as if they were marching not only towards Mount Cristou, but away from the present.

She had never seen a place where there were no signs of the modern world. Even back in Minnesota, where the plains stretched on unbroken for miles, there were bits of man's handiwork to remind a visitor that the land had been tamed. Cars. Telephone poles. Houses.

But there was none of that here; there was just this ribbon of dirt stretching towards the mountains. And it was eerily free of other travellers. They hadn't seen or even heard anyone since those awful moments in the forest.

A little shiver danced up Dorian's spine. She'd asked Jake who those men were, just before they'd started walking towards Kadar.

'Were they bandits, do you think?'

His answer had not been encouraging. 'One side's the same as the other, as far as we're concerned,' he'd said grimly.

She was more than willing to agree. If hearing those guttural voices hadn't been enough to convince her that Jake had been telling her the truth all along, then the feel of this strange countryside would have done it. Maybe it wasn't the sort of proof reporters were supposed to look for, but then, some of the best journalists she knew talked about having a 'nose for news', which was just another way of saying they'd learned to trust their instincts.

Dorian sighed. Actually, hers hadn't been too dependable lately. Kadar, by the looks of things, was certainly more than a couple of hours' walk. And if she'd waited for the search party she'd been sure was coming, those men would have found her by now.

But staying behind hadn't been an option. Jake had come back prepared to take her off the plane by force, if necessary. Would he have done that? she wondered. Her gaze moved over him as he strode along the road ahead of her. Yes. Yes, he would have. He would have tossed her over his shoulder or tied her and gagged her: he would have done whatever he damned well had to do to get what he wanted. For all that earlier sophisticated polish, Jake Prince was a man clearly in his element. Dorian smiled a little, remembering that she'd thought he might be Jack Alexander.

He wasn't, of course; she knew that now. Not just because he'd denied it—if Jack Alexander had been travelling incognito, he'd never admit it to a reporter— but because the last few hours had been convincing proof. The head of Barovnian Exports would be a man at home in skyscrapers and penthouses, a man used to the power of the boardroom and the pleasures of the bedroom, and the thought of him enduring in surroundings such as these was almost enough to make her laugh out loud.

But Jake—Jake was at home here. Not that she wasn't damned sure he was as familiar with the boardroom as Jack Alexander. That air of cool authority could only belong to a man accustomed to being in charge.

As for women—Dorian's gaze moved over him again. The afternoon had grown warm, and he'd taken off his leather jacket and stuffed it into the sack he carried. His shirt, damp with sweat, clung to his body, moulding itself to his shoulders and back so that it accentuated the play of muscle beneath his skin.

Suddenly, unexpectedly, she remembered how it had felt to be in his arms, to taste his mouth, to feel his heart beating against hers...

'...what you're feeling, Dorian.'

She looked up, startled. Jake was standing dead ahead, his hands on his hips, watching her with a narrow-eyed intensity that sent her pulse rocketing.

'What?'

'I said, if you don't answer my questions and let me know how you're feeling, you won't be able to blame me for pushing you too hard.'

The breath puffed from her lungs. 'Did you—did you ask me a question?'

He nodded. 'I asked if you wanted to take a five-minute break.'

Tell him you don't need to, she thought—but what was the sense in being stupid? She nodded, and Jake pointed to some flat rocks off to the side of the road.

'Are you all right?' he said when he sank down beside her.

She wasn't. There was a persistent ache in her right foot, but somehow the thought of admitting weakness to Jake was worse than enduring the growing discomfort.

'Fine,' she said with a quick smile.

She watched as he slipped the sack from his shoulder and unzipped it. Water, she thought, please, let there be a Thermos of water inside.

Jake held his hand. 'Have a piece of chocolate.'

She shook her head and opted for honesty. 'I'd rather have something to drink.'

'Later. For now, eat the chocolate.'

She had a sudden vision of that moment when he'd packed the sack. 'Soda,' she said. He looked up. 'There are some cans of Coke in there. I saw you put them in.'

He nodded as he unwrapped the chocolate. 'Yes. Maybe we'll open one later.'

'Why? I mean, if we're thirsty now——'

'*We* are not thirsty now,' he said coldly.

Dorian drew in her breath. 'OK,' she said, 'OK, *we're* not. *I* am. Do you want me to—to prostrate myself for a miserable drink?'

His expression grew very still. 'That's the second time you've accused me of being a petty dictator,' he said softly.

Her eyes met his. 'If the shoe fits...'

'The fact is, we may have a better use for those cans.'

She laughed tiredly. 'Be sure and let me know what it is when you figure it out, will you?'

'There's a village just ahead,' he said, ignoring her gibe. 'I want to be long past it by nightfall.'

'Nightfall?'

'Yes. We'll camp in the foothills.'

'But—but...'

'But what?' He smiled unpleasantly. 'Surely you didn't think we'd cross those mountains and reach Kadar today?'

She hadn't thought, and she didn't want to, even now. A night, spent in this desolate place? A night alone, just she and Jake? A tremor went through her, of fear and of something more.

'Tomorrow, then. We'll be at Kadar tomorrow,' she said quickly. 'Right?'

Jake gave her a long, steady look, and then he zipped the sack shut and stood up.

'Ready to go?'

'No...'

Dorian sighed. He was already striding down the narrow road. She rose slowly and dusted off the seat of her trousers with her hand. 'If you don't answer my questions... you won't be able to blame me for pushing. you too hard,' he'd said, but he hadn't meant it. She stared after him, tempted, for the moment, to call him back and tell him she needed a longer rest.

But she had no wish to show any signs of vulnerability to a man as unfeeling as Jake Prince. Instead, she firmed her jaw and fell in behind him.

*   *   *

She was debating whether it would be better to take off the miserable shoe and go barefoot by the time Jake announced another halt. She smothered a groan as she collapsed to the ground and kicked off the offending shoe.

'What's wrong?'

His voice was sharp. With concern, she thought in surprise—but then she looked up and saw the way he was watching her. It wasn't concern at all. Not for her, anyway. He was just worried that she'd put them off schedule.

'Nothing,' she said, defiance glinting in her eyes.

Jake cursed as he dropped the sack to the ground and squatted beside her.

'Let me see your foot,' he said angrily, pushing her hand aside.

She caught her breath when he touched his fingers lightly to the tender flesh, and then he sat back on his heels and glared at her.

'When did this happen?' he demanded.

'Don't worry about it.'

'I asked you a question, dammit.'

'You asked me one before, too. "Are you ready to go?" you said, but you didn't wait around to hear my answer.'

Jake looked at her in silence, then got to his feet. 'Get up.'

She moaned softly. 'Not yet. Please, let me just——' She gasped as he swung her up into his arms. 'What are you doing? I can walk.'

'And you will,' he growled as he strode into the trees that grew beside the road, 'after we take care of your foot. The village I told you about is just over that rise. I'm going to leave you for a while and go on ahead.'

'Leave me?' The thought was terrifying. 'No. Don't do that.'

He shifted her weight in his arms. 'I won't be gone long.'

'Jake, please—let me go with you.'

'It's out of the question.'

'Why?' Her gaze swept across his face, taking in the grim set to his mouth, the harsh thrust of jaw, and those cold, determined eyes. 'Just give me one good reas——'

'OK. One, your foot hurts and you might as well rest now as later, and——'

'But I'll manage.'

'And two,' he said, ducking his head as he made his way through a thicket of flowering wild cherry, 'we made a deal, you and I. I said I'd take you with me to Kadar—and you promised to do as you were told.'

'I did not. I said I'd do what seemed sensible,' she said quickly. 'And it isn't sensible to leave me alone here.'

He came to a stop and looked down at her, his eyes steady on her face.

'Are you afraid?' he asked softly.

'No,' she said quickly. 'No, of course not. I just—I just...'

'Nothing will happen to you here, Dorian.'

'You can't guarantee that, Jake. Anyone might——'

'I'll check the area thoroughly.'

'But why must you leave me here?'

He smiled. 'Do you speak Pragavic?'

She shook her head. 'No.'

He smiled again. 'I didn't think so.'

'Yes, but—but I could keep still. I wouldn't have to say anything.'

His smile became a grin. 'You? Somehow, that's hard to imagine.'

'I would, though. They'd never suspect that——'

'Of course they would.' His hand slipped up and cupped the back of her head. 'Your hair, Dorian. Your eyes—you're different. Everything about you is different.'

He was different, too, she thought suddenly. She had never known a man like him, a man at home in two such different worlds. She had never known a man who looked like him, either, with a hard masculinity that seemed only to enhance his beauty. Because he *was* beautiful. That tall, regal bearing. The handsome face, with its faint layer of dark stubble. And his eyes—she could see them clearly now. She had thought they were black, or even brown, but they weren't. They were something in between, a dark, midnight hazel that—that...

Say something, she told herself. Say anything.

But it was Jake who spoke, his voice low and intimate. 'Do you really want to be with me?'

It seemed hard to draw breath into her lungs. She had been afraid of being left alone when she'd made her admission, wondering who—or what—was in the woods. But Jake's whispered question had given her words an entirely different meaning and suddenly the air became charged with electricity.

That he'd still try and play such a game in the midst of danger infuriated her.

But that she felt herself responding to it infuriated her even more.

'I—I...' She drew a deep breath. 'Of course. That way, I can get some background information about—about the people in this place. For my articles, I mean.'

Jake's face changed to stone. 'How conscientious you are,' he said coldly. He lowered her to her feet and stepped back. 'Stay here and don't move. Not an inch, do you understand?'

'But—how long will you be gone?'

His smile was quick and humourless. 'As long as it takes,' he said, and then, like a shadowy ghost, he melted into the trees and vanished.

In truth, he wasn't gone very long at all. And when he did reappear he seemed to materialise out of nowhere.

'Here,' he said, dropping a bundle of clothing in her lap. 'Get those things on, and be quick about it.'

She frowned. 'What is all this?'

'What does it look like?' he snapped. 'A skirt and blouse. A shawl. And a pair of sandals. Come on, will you? We've only another couple of hours of daylight.'

She rose slowly. 'Where did you get this stuff?'

'From one of the village belles.' A cool smile twisted across his lips. 'Not your style, hmm?'

'But why? My clothing is torn, but it's still wearable.'

Jake laughed. 'I know this is going to break your heart,' he said, 'but truthfully I didn't give much thought to whether or not your outfit needed replacing.'

'Well, then . . .?'

'You look different from the women we'll see.'

That was what he'd said just a little while ago. But the words had had a softness then. Now, it was an indictment.

'We haven't seen anybody yet.'

'We will, once we reach the mountains, and the fact that you don't speak either Pragavic or Barovnian——'

'Barovnian?' She shook her head. 'Why would anyone expect me to speak that?'

'I can take care of that by saying my wife is mute,' he said, ignoring her. 'But the rest is impossible.'

Dorian's eyes widened. 'Mute?'

'Maybe we can get away with the colour of your hair and eyes,' he said thoughtfully. 'My country is small, and has been invaded often.' His eyes swept over her and a look of faint distaste settled on his face. 'But there's no way to explain your Western clothes—especially that trouser suit.'

'Jake, for heaven's sake—why will you have to make excuses for anything once we get to Barovnia?'

'We're wasting time,' he said in clipped tones. 'Change your clothing.'

'But—but you haven't explained anything.'

He caught hold of her shoulders. 'Dress yourself, Dorian, or I'll do it for you.'

Their eyes met and held. A flush of anger rose along her cheeks and she shrugged free of him.

'You really belong in this part of the world,' she said coldly. 'It suits you perfectly.'

His smile was grim. 'Does it?'

'Oh, yes. All that charm is just a cover-up, isn't it? You'd much rather give a woman orders than anything else.'

'You're wrong.'

Dorian tossed her head. 'I don't think so.'

'But you are.' He laughed softly as he reached out and caught her face in his hands. 'Giving a woman orders is sometimes necessary, but there are other things I much prefer doing.'

Colour flooded her cheeks again. 'I wonder,' she said evenly, 'does Jack Alexander know what kind of cold-hearted bastard you are?'

Jake's smile vanished, like a light suddenly extinguished.

'He knows all there is to know about me, Dorian.'

'And he still wants you around?' She grimaced. 'But then, why wouldn't he? He's probably the same kind of rat you are.'

'No.' His voice was very soft, almost a whisper. 'He isn't. He's far worse than I am.' He looked at her for a long moment, and then he let go of her and turned away. 'You have two minutes to get out of what you're wearing and into the clothes I've given you.' He glanced down at his watch. 'Two minutes, Dorian.'

She stared at his back, at the straight spine, the arrogantly held head, and she knew that he meant what he said.

Her fingers flew over buttons and hooks, until her khaki suit lay at her feet and she was dressed in the soft black wool skirt, embroidered blouse, and dark leather sandals Jake had brought for her.

The clothing fitted well enough; it was even handsome, in its own way. Why, then, did it make her feel so uncomfortable?

'Thirty seconds, Dorian. Twenty. Ten——'

'I'm ready,' she said quickly.

Jake turned around, his gaze moving slowly over her. She felt it linger at the slight swell of her breasts visible in the scooped neckline of the blouse, felt it feather across the narrow waist of the skirt. When he looked up, he was smiling.

'Yes,' he said softly, 'yes, you'll do. You'll do fine.' She watched as he buried her khaki suit and shoes underneath a rock. 'Now, let's see that foot.'

She started to tell him that her foot would be OK in the thick-soled sandals, but one glance at his determined face and she knew it would be useless to argue.

'It's fine,' she said, propping her foot on his knee as he knelt before her.

Jake pulled a strip of soft flannel from the sack, made a pad of it, and slipped it between the sole of her foot and the sandal. His hands were strong, yet surprisingly gentle. Without warning, she thought of how they would feel on her breasts...

'All right.' He rose quickly. 'Let's go. I don't think we'll cross anyone's path until morning, but, if we do, remember who you are.'

She stiffened, reacting as much to the unexpected vision of a moment ago as to his air of authority.

'This is ridiculous,' she said. 'I don't have to——'

'You are mute.' His voice was harsh. 'And you are my wife. Do you understand?'

'No, dammit, I do not understand.'

'There's no time for explanations. Just do as you're told.'

'Why?' Her eyes flashed green sparks. 'Because that's how the men of your country treat their women?'

Jake's eyes narrowed. 'That's as good a reason as any.'

'Well, I have news for you, Jake Prince. You may belong in this part of the world, but I don't. And I am not your woman. I——'

She cried out as he reached for her and pulled her into his arms. His mouth dropped to hers and he kissed her with a harsh, unforgiving passion that left her breathless.

'You are what I say you are, until we reach Kadar,' he said when he lifted his head. 'Is that clear?'

She blinked back the angry tears that rose in her eyes. 'Absolutely.'

He gave her a long, steady look, and then he nodded and turned away.

'Let's go, then,' he said and, after a moment, because there really weren't any other choices, Dorian fell in behind him.

CHAPTER SEVEN

DORIAN blotted her forehead with a corner of her shawl, spat out a mouthful of dust, and did her damnedest to keep up with Jake.

None of it was easy. The shawl was getting soggy with sweat, she felt as if she'd swallowed half the dirt road, and Jake—Jake was marching along as if he didn't care whether she could stay with him or not.

No. That wasn't exactly true. He'd asked her, when they'd started, if her foot felt all right, and he'd asked the same question half a dozen times since in a way that implied that he expected her to be the worst kind of burden.

'It's fine,' she'd kept saying, which was true enough. The improvised pad, and the thick leather sandals, had solved the problem. Eventually, he'd stopped asking. Now, he simply glanced back from time to time, checking her presence the way you would check to see if a stray dog was still following you.

'Let's go, let's go. Can't you move any faster?'

She glared at his sweat-soaked back. No, she thought, not without wings. I'm exhausted and sweaty and I hate you for what you've done to me, dressing me in this—this cheap costume out of a bad operetta, treating me as if I were your property, making veiled references to danger ahead when the truth was the danger was long past, and all because you're determined to make me look and feel foolish.

Her mouth tightened. God, how she ached to tell him all that and more. Jake Prince was a man with no heart

90

and no feelings. He was a robot, damn him; that was why he could keep such a killing pace.

But why would she give him the satisfaction of telling him what he already knew? He *knew* he held all the cards until they reached Kadar; she had to follow where he led and do what he ordered, her only comfort the knowledge of what she would write when she finally got to a typewriter.

Jake Prince, a barbarian in a barbaric land, gives new meaning to the word 'uncivilised'. If Jack Alexander has any plans to bring Barovnia into the twenty-first century, he would be well-advised to oust Mr Prince from his circle of advisers ...

And if that's what Jake was, then Alexander was a fool.

'Come on, Oliver. Your feet are dragging.'

Dorian looked up. Jake was standing on the road ahead, glaring at her, his hands planted firmly on his hips.

More than her feet were dragging, but she'd be damned if she'd let him know that.

'What's dragging is these sandals. Do all the women in this God-forsaken place have feet the size of ox carts?'

'Be grateful I got you sandals at all.' His gaze raked over her. 'And get that shawl up on your head.'

'It's wool. It's too warm to wear in this sun.'

'Get it on. You're supposed to look like a peasant.'

'I am sweating to death under this thing,' she said when she reached him. She yanked the shawl from her shoulders. 'Look, if you don't believe me.'

Jake smiled coldly. 'What's the matter, Oliver? Haven't you ever worked up an honest sweat before?'

'You don't know——'

'But then, you wouldn't have to, would you? Sitting at a desk all day, wielding a poison pen, isn't very taxing.'

'I see. Now I'm going to get a lecture on the honesty and decency of physical labour.' She glared at him as she shoved her damp hair behind her ears. 'Well, before you get carried away, I suggest you consider what *you* do for a living as opposed to what you might be doing.'

His face darkened as he caught her shoulders. 'What in hell is that supposed to mean?' he demanded.

'You're hurting me!'

'Answer the question, Dorian. What did you mean?'

'Just that I doubt very much if being an adviser to a man like Jack Alexander improves the condition of the world any more than my work does,' she said as she twisted in his grasp.

He stared at her for another few seconds and then he dropped his hands to his sides. When he spoke, she could hear a faint weariness in his voice.

'Just get that thing on your head.'

'Come on, Jake. We haven't seen a soul. Anyway, you didn't worry about what I was wearing before.'

'There were no alternatives before. Now pull the shawl up.'

'But——'

'Dammit, woman, are you a slow learner or just a fool?' He took a quick step towards her until they were only inches apart. 'Good wives are not argumentative. And ones who are mute are not argumentative at all.'

'That's ridiculous. There's no one here to——'

Jake reached out and caught her by the wrist. 'You are my woman, Dorian,' he said in a harsh whisper. 'And women know their place here. Do you understand—or must I give you a lesson?'

Tears of rage and frustration glistened in her eyes. 'I hate you, Jake, do you know that?'

His smile was grim. 'Hearing that just about breaks my heart. Now, get that scarf up over your head. Further. Further, dammit.' When it hung down over her forehead, half covering her eyes, he nodded with satisfaction. 'Keep it that way,' he said, and he swung away from her and set off towards the mountains again.

She stared after him, hating not just him, but his long-legged stride and the dirt and the itchy shawl, too.

'You just wait until I file my first dispatch,' she called out. 'You just wait...'

Jake didn't bother turning around. Why would he? Her threat was meaningless. They were miles from a telephone or fax machine. Besides, he'd said he would censor whatever she tried to send out, and the more time she spent with him, the more certain she was that he had the power to do it.

For the time being, at least, he was in command.

Grim-faced, she marched on.

The road grew narrower. It began to slope upwards, the angle increasing steadily. Dorian was breathing hard now, even panting a little, and her legs ached. Jake had to know that she was pushing herself to the limit and beyond, but he didn't slow down or give any quarter.

That was OK, she thought darkly. She could keep it up as long as he did, and if she needed anything to keep her going all she had to do was remember what he'd said about being his woman until they reached Kadar. And if that didn't do the trick, remembering how he'd kissed her certainly would.

Her mouth still felt the imprint of that kiss. It had been bruising, even degrading. It was a kiss that had had nothing to do with passion and everything to do with dominance. It had been a graphic, almost brutal reminder of her status.

She was a woman, dependent for her survival on a man she barely knew, in a place that time had forgotten.

Well, she had a message for Jake Prince. He could swathe her in wool like a badly wrapped package, he could treat her with disdain, he could pretend that they'd both fallen into the thirteenth century—but she was still herself inside, where it really counted. She was Dorian Oliver, and she could handle whatever he dished out.

Suddenly, it became important not just to follow ten paces to the rear, as she had all morning, but to match Jake stride for stride. Her footsteps quickened until she was at his side. Jake gave her a quick glance and if she hadn't been breathing so hard she would have laughed aloud at the look on his face.

'You'd be better off behind me,' he said.

'I'm better off right where I am,' she puffed, and she slogged along beside him, gritting her teeth and letting her hatred for Jake give her the strength to continue.

And it worked, even after her legs turned to lead and her lungs to flame. It worked, even when Jake plunged off the dirt road on to a twisting trail where the brambles and tree branches seemed determined to draw blood from any patch of exposed skin. After a while, she had to drop back because the trail was only wide enough for one, but that was just as well.

She was completely exhausted and disorientated. Her eyes focused singularly on the path at her feet while she tried not to think about her aching muscles, thirst, and...

'*Bognia dovitch*?'

The guttural voice startled her and she went careering into Jake's back. She collected herself, stood on tiptoe, and peered over his shoulder.

Ahead of him—oh, lord—ahead of him were two of the biggest, most wicked-looking men she had ever seen. They wore trousers and shirts similar to Jake's, but theirs were encrusted with filth. Knives with sharp, curving blades gleamed in their waistbands.

Her eyes went from the fat one with the piggy face to the tall, broad one with the moustache. Quickly, she covered her face with the shawl so that only her eyes showed.

'*Saletsa*?' Pig Face said, and, although she had no idea what the word meant, the way he was looking at her terrified her.

Jake said something to the men in that same rough tongue, and then he reached back and grasped her wrist, snarling something guttural to her as he dragged her up to stand beside him. She shook her head and all three men laughed.

Dorian's heart fluttered. The sun was dipping towards the horizon, but she knew that wasn't why she suddenly felt so cold. She looked past Jake. Pig Face was grinning at her. She cast her eyes down, glad to be wrapped in concealing layers of dark wool.

The conversation went on and on, and she needed no translator to warn her that parts of it were about her. Jake was laughing as much as the strangers were; she caught her breath when his hand left her wrist and moved casually over her body.

'*Shnoi voritch*,' he said, and she knew that he was staking claim to her.

'*You are my woman, until we reach Kadar.*'

The words that had so angered her hours before were her only solace now. But—would the deception work?

Jake barked a command at her, put his hand into the small of her back, and shoved her forward. Pig Face laughed as she brushed past him, her eyes cast obediently towards her sandals. Jake barked again and she came to a halt, waiting, trembling, watching out of the corner of her eye as he and the strangers grasped each other's forearms. The two men strode off, vanishing down the trail, and Jake moved up towards her.

'*Gastia*,' he snarled as he elbowed past her, and she fell in dutifully behind him.

She made no attempt to catch up to him this time. Instead, she shuffled along, eyes downcast, trying to breathe past the lump in her throat that was her stomach, trying not to look back over her shoulder to see if Pig Face and his friend had really vanished. Time dragged by, an hour, perhaps more, until finally, *finally*, Jake stopped and turned around.

'Wait,' he said softly.

She watched as he trotted down the trail. There was nothing but silence; then, just when she'd almost given up hope, he reappeared.

'It's OK,' he said. 'They're gone.'

'Gone?' she whispered.

Jake nodded. 'Yes.'

A sob of relief burst from her throat. 'Oh, God,' she whispered. 'Jake—Jake...'

He caught hold of her. 'It's all right, kitten,' he said softly. 'Everything is OK now.'

She wanted to answer, to say something clever—one of the one-liners she did so well—but all that came out of her was another sob. Jake looked at her for a long moment, his dark eyes sweeping over her face, and then he sighed and drew her close to him.

'Come here,' he said gruffly.

His arms tightened around her and she burrowed against him, seeking the warmth and strength that were so much a part of him. She was safe now, she would be safe so long as he held her.

How could that be? the journalistic sceptic within her whispered, but Dorian was too drained to care.

The moments ticked away like heartbeats, and then Jake drew the shawl from her head and let it fall to her shoulders.

'I've pushed you hard,' he said.

Dorian wanted to laugh. What was the point in denying it, when they both knew that it was his arms and his strength that were keeping her on her feet?

'A little,' she whispered.

He sighed. 'I had no choice, kitten. This was the only safe place I could think of to spend the night.'

She looked up, noticing their surroundings for the first time. They were in what seemed to be a rocky bowl. Grey stone slabs rose all around them.

The place looked desolate, but strangely enough it gave her a feeling of comfort—until she remembered.

'Jake.' Dorian gave a little shudder. 'Those men...'

He drew her head to his chest. 'Don't think about them.'

How could she not think of them? She would never forget them, not as long as she lived.

'But—will they come after us?'

'They'd have trouble finding this spot, I think.' She felt the rise and fall of his chest and he chuckled softly. 'Besides, I doubt that they're much interested in you any more.'

'They were, though.' She drew back and looked at him. 'I knew it!'

'Uh-huh. So I told them they could have you.'

Her mouth dropped open. 'You did what?'

He laughed at the look on her face. 'I said you were all theirs—if they really had use for a woman who had no teeth.'

'No teeth?' she said in horror. Her fingers went to her mouth.

'And no nose.' He smiled modestly. 'Hell, kitten, I thought that was a nice touch. A woman with no teeth is one thing, but a woman without a nose...'

Dorian swallowed. 'I—I don't understand,' she whispered. 'No nose? No teeth?'

'I told them I'd cut your nose off myself.'

'But—but why would they believe you?'

'Because that's still the penalty for adultery among some of the hill tribes.' He grinned. 'I said I'd knocked out most of your teeth for disobedience before that, and you really weren't much of a beauty any more, and that was why I was taking you to the bridal market at Quarem where I could, perhaps, sell you to a blind man—unless they wanted to buy you now and save me the trip.'

'And—and they didn't,' she said shakily.

Jake's smile turned grim. 'No. Fortunately for us, they didn't.'

'But—but how—you can't mean things like that still happen?'

He let out a deep sigh. 'It's not easy to take a country from the Dark Ages into the future,' he said. 'People— and customs—lag behind.' There was a moment's silence, and then he stepped back and smiled at her. 'Now,' he said briskly, 'how about supper?'

Dorian sighed. 'Do we still have some chocolate left?'

He nodded as he eased the sack from his shoulder and dropped it to the ground.

'Chocolate,' he said, digging into it. 'A packet of mints.' He looked up and grinned. 'Two boiled potatoes. Two hard-boiled eggs. And a loaf of black bread.'

'That stuff wasn't on the plane.'

Jake chuckled. 'You didn't really think that high-fashion outfit you're wearing was a two-Coke job, did you? I traded one can of soda for this feast.'

She smiled as she plopped down beside him. 'It *is* a feast,' she said. 'I'm starved.'

He handed her a potato. 'How's your foot?'

'My foot? Oh, it's fine.'

'Are you sure?'

'Uh-huh. These shoes did the trick.'

He smiled wryly. 'The ox carts, you mean?'

Dorian smiled, too, and then she cleared her throat. 'Jake?' She hesitated. 'What—what's Barovnia like?'

His smiled faded. 'I thought you knew what it was like. Backward. Barbaric. Primitive.'

Patches of colour rose to her cheeks. 'I guess I deserve that. But I only got this assignment a couple of hours before I was due at the airport. And, you've got to admit, Barovnia's not a country that's in the news very much.'

'You mean, it isn't a household name.'

'Well . . .' She looked at him, relaxing as she saw his lips twitch in a faint smile. 'Exactly. I doubt if most people had ever heard of it, until the death of the *abdhan*.'

'You're right.' He sighed as he picked up an egg and began shelling it. 'And it's ironic as hell—I mean, the old man spent his entire life doing his damnedest to keep Barovnia out of the world's eye, and now...'

Dorian pulled a slice of dark bread from the small round loaf. 'Did you know him?' she asked softly.

Jake nodded. 'Yes.'

'What was he like?'

He shrugged. 'Dedicated to his people; a believer in the old ways... I didn't know him all that well, actually. I hadn't seen him in years. Not since I was a boy.'

'And the new *abdhan*, the one who's been hurt? Do you know him, too?'

There was a silence before he spoke. When he did, his voice was gruff.

'Seref and I were playmates when we were kids.'

'Then you must be very worried about him,' Dorian said stiffly.

Jake nodded. 'Yes. Being cut off like this, without any way to find out how he is...' Suddenly, his eyes turned cool. He gave her a long, steady look, and then a tight smile angled across his mouth. 'You're good at this,' he said softly.

She stared at him. 'Good at what?'

'It's quite a technique, Miss Oliver.' He gathered together the remnants of their meal, then got to his feet. 'The sweetly concerned voice, the innocent face—I suppose I should be grateful you don't have a tape recorder tucked into your pocket.'

It took a few seconds to realise what he meant. Once she did, Dorian rose quickly and hurried after him.

'You're wrong, Jake,' she said honestly. 'I wasn't even thinking about *WorldWeek* just now. I was just interested in——'

'I'm sure it works like a charm most of the time—especially on men.' His tone was clipped; he was moving quickly, deeper and deeper into the rock-strewn valley, peering into shadowed clefts as he spoke. 'But I can promise you that it won't work again.'

'Jake, please——' She gasped as he whirled around and caught her by the shoulders.

'I told you before, Dorian. Don't push me. And don't underestimate my intelligence, either.'

'I wasn't. I mean, I didn't. I just...' She ran her tongue along her lips. She really hadn't been thinking of the magazine at all while they'd been talking. That, in itself, was troubling; why hadn't she been taking mental notes for a later article? 'I wasn't thinking of *World Week*,' she said honestly. 'I suppose—I was only trying to make sense of things. Try and see it my way, will you? Yesterday, I was in New York, where everything was familiar, and now—now...'

'Now, you're in the middle of nowhere with a man who could give you the interview you're longing for.'

'Jake, please——'

'Just how far would you go to get that interview?'

His voice had gone soft, not with promise but with menace. She felt her pulse give a nervous flutter, but she forced herself to meet his gaze head-on.

'Let go of me,' she said quietly.

'Just think of the article you could write. "Innocent girl reporter, raped by Barovnian barbarian..." Or would it really be rape, Dorian?' His teeth flashed as he gathered her against him; she felt the quick, hard heat of his body against hers. 'No,' he said softly, 'I don't think it would.'

'I know what you're trying to do, Jake.'

He laughed. 'I'd be disappointed if you didn't.'

'You're just—you're just trying to scare me.' He was succeeding, too, she thought shakily, but she couldn't afford to let him know that. 'We both know Jake Prince isn't the kind of man who'd——'

Jake laughed again. 'You don't know a damned thing about Jake Prince.'

'I know that the man I met back in New York wouldn't use sex as a weapon.'

'No.' His mouth twisted. 'But that's not who I am any more, Dorian. I'm someone else entirely, someone who doesn't have to live by any laws but his own.'

'Are you telling me I was right, then?' It was getting hard to keep her voice steady. 'Are you saying that Barovnians are animals?'

He went very still. She waited, barely breathing, while the seconds dragged by, forcing herself not to look away from his flat, cold stare. Then, with no change of expression, he let go of her and stepped back.

'It will be dark soon. We'd better get settled in.'

She watched as he turned and began making his way up the sloping hillside. She was shaking now, in the aftermath of the last awful moments. It was impossible to really think he'd have taken her by force, but the tautly controlled violence in him had been real enough; it had been basic, almost primitive, and it had stunned her.

'Let's go,' he called, his voice rough with impatience. 'In another few minutes you won't be able to see an inch beyond your nose.'

She blinked. He was right: the sky was already a soft charcoal against which the rocks stood out in dark—and threatening—relief.

Dorian blew out her breath and started climbing up towards him.

'Can't we build a fire?' she said.

Jake shook his head. 'Not unless you want guests dropping in for a cup of coffee.'

No, she thought with a shudder as she followed after him while he peered into dark crevasses and under rocky ledges, she certainly did not. When finally he grunted his approval, she was glad to see that he'd picked a spot protected on three sides by large boulders.

'This should do,' he said, tossing the two small blankets to her. 'Put one of those under you—the ground is still chilly this time of year.'

'Won't you need one?'

He shook his head. 'I have my jacket. It's enough.'

He dropped to the ground, ignoring her completely. She watched as he leaned back against a boulder, crossed his long legs at the ankle, and tucked his hands into his armpits.

Dorian sighed. She spread one of the blankets on the ground, lay down on it, and draped the second blanket over herself. Jake was right about the chill; within minutes, she felt it seeping into her bottom and into her legs. She rolled on to her belly, wrapping herself in the blanket, trying to find a bit of ground that didn't have sharp rocks protruding from the soil.

He'd been right about nightfall, too. Darkness had swallowed them up; it was a moonless, starless night, and the blackness was so complete that it was almost disorientating.

Where was Pig Face? she wondered suddenly.

Far from here, she hoped. Very far from here.

Something shifted stealthily just below them. There was the scrabble of claws, a faint stirring sound, a tiny squeal.

'Jake?' she whispered.

He sighed. 'It's probably a mouse, Dorian, and it's not the least bit interested in us. Just shut your eyes and get some sleep.'

She rolled on to her side and cradled her head on her arms. He was right. She needed sleep—she was exhausted, weary to the very marrow of her bones. And tomorrow wouldn't be any easier. Tomorrow...

An animal cried out into the night, its voice rising like the shriek of a demented soul in torment. Dorian gasped and struggled upright.

'Jake? Did you hear that?'

'Lord.' His voice was hoarse with weariness. 'It was a wild dog.'

'No dog in the world ever——'

'A wolf, then. They hunt at night. Now lie back.'

'A wolf?' Her voice rose into the darkness. 'A wolf? Are you serious?'

'Oh, for God's sake!' Jake's arm snaked out and wound around her waist. 'Come here,' he demanded, tugging her towards him, 'and shut up so we can both get some rest.'

'I can't,' she whispered.

He turned her to him and drew her closer, until she was lying back in the protective curve of his arm, her body pressed against the hard warmth of his.

'You can. Count chickens or sheep—or covers of *WorldWeek*, with your byline on it,' he added drily. 'Think about whatever will comfort you enough so you can sleep.'

'Nothing will. I—I...'

Dorian yawned. Lord, she was so tired. Beside her, Jake's breathing slowed; she felt the warmth of it soft against her temple. How could he have fallen asleep so easily? 'Count sheep,' he'd said. Sheep. Or bylines. Or *WorldWeek* covers.

Covers. Covers, with her name prominently displayed...

Long moments later, she was still awake. It wasn't going to work. Think about whatever was comforting, Jake had said, but Jake didn't—he didn't...

Think about whatever was comforting.

Dorian's eyelids drooped. Jake, she thought dreamily, Jake...

And then she was asleep.

CHAPTER EIGHT

IN JAKE PRINCE'S Footsteps: a first-person account of an impossible journey, by Dorian Oliver, WorldWeek Magazine. Entry One: we go through the Cristou Mountains via the Tomma Pass...

The sun beat down on the trail that wound like a grey ribbon towards the cleft that divided the massive mountain. High overhead, vultures wheeled in the sky, waiting and watching for any creature that might succumb to a mis-step or to the sudden death of an avalanche.

Dorian tried not to think about that. She tried, too, not to think about the way her breath was wheezing in and out of her lungs or how the muscles in her calves burned with fire. And she tried most especially not to think about how far they'd come or how far they had yet to walk.

What was the point? Jake wouldn't give a damn if she fell on her face; he'd only stand over her and tell her to either get moving or be left behind...

And if she really knew how many endless miles they had yet to cover, she might just do that.

The one thing she wasn't concentrating on was the scenery. Not that it wasn't spectacular: the craggy mountain peaks rising around her, still gleaming under snowy mantles, the puffy clouds that seemed close enough to touch, the occasional glimpse of a white-bearded mountain goat—it was all beautiful, even exotic. But you had to lift your head to really get a look at things, and lifting your head took energy.

Dorian had little energy left.

Jake, damn the man, had enough for both of them. He was still moving along ahead of her as if he were out for a morning's stroll, just as he had been from the beginning, his easy stride effortlessly eating up the miles.

Air puffed in and out between her parted lips.

Entry Two: We will be at the Barovnian border soon, according to Jake. Up this slope, then down the other side, and—finally—we will be in Kadar, although I keep thinking of what Jake said yesterday, about my keeping mute once we reach his country. I must have misunderstood him. I would ask, but my reluctant guide and I have not spoken in hours...

It had been early morning when exhaustion, hunger and a night spent sleeping on the rocky ground had combined to produce the kind of disorientation that had led to the incident that had ended in their mutual silence.

She had come awake slowly, rising from a deep, peaceful sleep.

'Mmm,' she'd murmured while she stretched languorously.

She ached—her back felt stiff, and so did her legs—but her head was comfortably cradled on a hard yet yielding pillow. There were noises in the background, not the distant sounds of traffic that penetrated her apartment windows almost twenty-four hours a day nor even the drone of the clock-radio. What she heard were bird calls, piercingly sweet and clear.

'Mmm,' she sighed as she snuggled more deeply into the warmth of her bed.

'Good morning, kitten.'

The voice was soft as silk, sweet as honey. Something touched her temple—a butterfly's wings, gentle and cool.

'Did you sleep well?'

Jake, her sleep-fogged brain whispered. Jake...

She came awake immediately, eyes opening wide and fastening on the dark, intense ones looking down into hers. Jake was holding her closely in his arms; her cheek was against his shoulder, her mouth almost at his throat. Her arm was curled around his waist. They were as intimately entwined as—as lovers, sharing the same space, even the same breath.

Waves of colour beat across her cheeks. God! Had they slept this way all night? Desperately, she tried to remember. The pitch-black night; the quavering bark of the wolf; Jake, pulling her into his arms...

Jake smiled. It was a slow, sexy smile, and it sent heat pulsing through her veins.

'I've never shared my bed with a kitten before.'

Had they...? Had she...? No. No, she would have remembered if Jake had made love to her. His kisses would have burned her flesh, his touch would have turned her body into flame.

His smile grew softer, hinting at secrets yet to be shared. 'You have a very expressive face, kitten,' he said in a hoarse whisper. His finger traced lightly along the contours of her mouth, and she had the sudden, almost overwhelming desire to touch her tongue to his skin and taste its heat. 'I can almost read your mind.'

'Jake.' Was that papery croak hers? 'Jake, please...'

'What?' He moved, tilting her head back, and smiled down at her. 'What were you going to ask me?'

His eyes were dark and filled with promise. His mouth was inches from hers. She remembered suddenly how he tasted: clean, smoky, cool. And she wanted—oh, she wanted...

He bent and brushed his lips over hers ever so lightly, the kiss like the touch of a butterfly's wings.

'Kitten.'

Dorian closed her eyes as his mouth found hers again. His lips moved on hers, seeking response; she whimpered as he shifted, rolling her gently so that she lay back against the warm earth. Their bodies touched, and she could feel his desire for her.

'Jake...'

'I want you,' he whispered. She caught her breath as his hand stroked her body. 'I've wanted you from the beginning, Dorian. You know that.'

And she wanted him. It was pointless to pretend she didn't. She'd wanted to be with him, to go with him that very first night...

His hand slipped under her blouse; she gasped as he cupped her breast. The heat of the sun was on her face, but it was the heat of Jake's fingers against her skin that set her trembling.

'Such a beautiful kitten,' he whispered. 'So soft, so sweet.' Her lips parted as his mouth closed on hers again. Their breath intermingled and Jake groaned and gathered her closer.

He kissed her deeply, passionately, while his fingers stroked her nipple. Her head fell back in supplication as he kissed the long column of her throat, the soft rise of her breast. Her body felt molten, as if it had been waiting for the moment when Jake's touch would shape it and claim it as his own.

'Do you want this?' he whispered, and she answered by sighing his name and linking her arms around his neck. She drew him down to her, her fingers tunnelling into his dark hair.

Somewhere high in the pale blue sky a bird of prey cried out in fierce exultation, its pagan cry mingling with Jake's growl of triumph as he moved over her.

'Tell me that you belong to me,' he said in a fierce whisper. 'Tell me that you are my woman.'

And, as suddenly as she had become fire in his arms, Dorian became stone.

'You are what I say you are, until we reach Kadar.'

The words—Jake's words—echoed inside her head. Oh, God, she thought, and she began to tremble, not with desire but with disgust for herself, for what she had almost let happen.

Jake lifted his head and looked down at her. 'Dorian?'

'Let me up,' she said quietly.

His eyes fixed on hers. 'Kitten—what's wrong?'

Everything, she thought. I've just behaved like a fool. No. I behaved like a—a slave-girl, being seduced by her master.

Years of trading verbal barbs as a journalist came to her rescue.

'You said you'd never awakened with a kitten in your arms, Jake,' she said coldly. 'Well, I've never awakened with a tomcat in mine—and it's a species I don't much care for.'

Jake went absolutely still. 'What is this all about, Dorian?'

'An experiment,' she said, forcing herself to meet his eyes. 'I thought it might be interesting to try——'

His hand closed lightly on her throat. 'Something different? Like a barbarian, perhaps?' His voice was deadly soft and dangerous.

'Let go of me,' Dorian had said calmly, although she knew he must feel the leap of her pulse under his fingers.

After a long, long moment he'd given her a cold, terrible smile.

'I am like the wolf, Dorian. Left to my own devices, I bother no one. But force my back against the wall, and you risk the danger of my fangs.'

It had taken all her courage to smile back. 'What is that, Jake, some quaint Barovnian proverb?'

'Simply a reminder of your own vulnerability.' While she'd still been struggling for a response, he'd rolled away from her and risen to his feet. 'Go on into the bushes and do whatever you have to do,' he'd said coldly, and she'd known that this, too, was a reminder—a reminder of their complete isolation. 'We've miles to cover before nightfall.'

They had not exchanged another word in the hours since, not even after they'd finally reached the mountain and begun climbing.

Entry Three: The mountains in this part of the world are like none I've ever seen. They are incredibly high and treacherous. Although the Tamma Pass has been a steady climb, the going has been uneventful—except when rockslides from past avalanches block the way, but I scramble over them behind Jake, clutching at rocks and boulders, sometimes falling back a step for each two I take. I long to ask how much further there is to go, but I won't. It's becoming like some awful game, waiting to see which of us will be the first to break the silence ...

'... if you need it.'

She looked up, startled by the sound of Jake's voice. He was standing a few yards away, looking back down the trail towards her, his face set, devoid of expression.

Dorian drew a deep, gasping breath. 'Sorry,' she said, pushing the hair from her eyes. 'I didn't quite get that.'

'I said, we can take a break, if you like. Unless you'd rather keep going...?'

She knew what he expected her to say, what her own pride told her to say. But she was beyond such foolishness; besides, she'd won the game of who-speaks-first, and that was enough for the day.

'I'd just as soon stop for a break,' she said, and without further hesitation she sank down into the grass, fell back, and closed her eyes. Moments later, she sighed. 'Do we have much further to go?'

'Another mile, perhaps. And then——'

'And then we'll be in Barovnia,' Dorian said, thinking how amazingly beautiful the name could sound when it marked the end of their journey.

She felt the brush of Jake's leg against hers as he sat down.

'Yes. Barovnia.'

She opened her eyes and looked up at him. His face was an emotionless mask, his voice without feeling, which was surprising for a man almost at the end of a difficult journey. She watched him from under her lashes.

He was sitting with his legs crossed beneath him, looking out over the valley, but she had the feeling that he wasn't really seeing any of it.

'Jake?' She hesitated. Would he be civil after what had happened this morning? Well, she had nothing to lose by trying. The worst he could do was give her more of the silent treatment. 'Jake? What's Kadar like?'

She was surprised to see a faint smile tilt across his mouth.

'Primitive,' he said.

Dorian bristled. 'Look, I've apologised and apologised——'

'I'm quite serious. I don't mean that it's uncivilised—my people's culture is ancient and beautiful, and the city itself is a handsome mix of old and new.' He sighed. 'But it hasn't the amenities it should have in today's world.' He looked at her. 'Oh, there's electricity, even a telephone service that works most of the time—but there aren't enough physicians or hospital beds, there are horse-drawn carts on the roads and veiled women in the streets...'

'Veiled women?' She shook her head. 'But Kadar is the capital of a European city, not a Middle Eastern one.'

Jake smiled thinly. 'There's a saying in my country: "Barovnia is the tie between the continents and the chasm that separates them."'

'"My people—my country."' Dorian looked at him. 'I don't think I've ever heard you say that before.'

'I told you, I was born there.'

'Yes. But somehow I thought you saw yourself as part of the West.'

'I'm an American,' he said sharply.

'And a Barovnian, as well?'

Jake shrugged. 'It's difficult to explain. Sometimes I feel—I feel...' He blew out his breath. 'I told you, it's hard to explain.'

'You don't have to. I understand.'

He laughed. 'No, you don't. How could you, when I don't understand it myself?'

'Well, I know how *I* feel, when I go home for a visit. I always wonder if it will feel strange to be in Minnesota again. Am I a mid-westerner, I think as the plane takes off, or am I an easterner?'

'And? Which are you?'

She smiled. 'I'm still trying to figure that out.'

Jake smiled, too. 'Somehow, I can't quite see you as a mid-west farm girl.'

'But I was, for almost nineteen years. And then...'

'And then?' he prompted, stretching out beside her and propping his head on his hand.

'And then,' she said with a little shrug, 'I decided to see if all those high-school English awards I'd won had any meaning. So I packed up my typewriter and headed east.'

'Where you found fame and fortune at *WorldWeek*,' he said.

'Where I found a weekly pay-cheque that would disgrace a beggar,' she said with deliberate lightness, 'and an old-boy system that might just let me wangle a byline in a hundred years or so.'

'And you decided to stay.'

She smiled wryly as she sat up and wrapped her arms around her knees. 'Of course.'

'Well, that's certainly logical,' Jake said with a little laugh. 'After all, if the pay's bad and the chance for advancement's even worse, what else could you have done?'

Dorian rested her head on her knees. 'What do you do for a living, Jake?'

There was a moment's silence. 'This and that,' he said finally. 'I'm in the export business.'

'And you're successful?'

He shrugged. 'I suppose you could say that, yes.'

'Did you work hard to get where you are?'

His mouth tightened. 'Some would say no.'

'But you say...?'

'I say—I say I took a small, family-owned company and made it into an international firm.'

She nodded. 'And was it easy?'

Jake laughed. 'Hell, no. It was hard work.'

'But you loved every minute of it?'

His eyes darkened with suspicion. 'What is this, Dorian? The game of twenty questions?'

'It's an explanation,' she said. 'I love what I do, the same as you. And I want to carve a niche for myself, the same as you.' She picked up a loose stone and examined it intently. 'And I will, some day. All I need is a chance.'

Silence fell over them, broken only by the soft whisper of the wind.

'I suppose you expect these reports you'll file from Barovnia will give you that chance,' Jake said finally.

Dorian lay back and rested her head on her arms. She had thought a lot about her dispatches while they were climbing through the pass, and the more she'd thought, the more she'd realised that what she'd write—what she'd *really* write, not the fanciful copy she'd composed in her head to make the time pass more quickly—would not, when you came down to it, be that different from everyone else's stuff.

Her assignment had been Jack Alexander. That was the simple truth of it. Walt Hemple had chosen her because he'd hoped she'd catch Alexander's eye, and, even if she'd balked against setting out to deliberately do that, she'd certainly hoped to interview the man.

But whatever chance she'd had was long gone. She'd spent the past two days a million miles from the next *abdhan*. He would have said all he had to say to the other reporters by now; they would have filed their stories, enough of them so that the Western Press was probably on overload. Anything she would write would only be superfluous.

Even Jake's solo flight, which had seemed so mysterious and promising, didn't seem that way any more. She still didn't know why he'd made it, but what did it matter? It was too late for it to have any effect on what was happening in Kadar. After all, if death had come to Barovnia's ruler and Jack Alexander was crowned *abdhan*, the ceremonies could certainly go on without Jake.

It was only this journey across the wilderness that might prove interesting—but not newsworthy. It had nothing whatsoever to do with the man of the hour.

The bottom line was that she was out of the action, and there was nothing she could do about it.

'Well? Is this Barovnian jaunt your ticket to success?' Jake's voice was rough with impatience. She looked up at him and smiled wearily.

'To tell you the truth, unless Jack Alexander suddenly fell into my lap with the offer of an exclusive interview, my stuff won't even raise an eyebrow in New York.'

Jake got to his feet and stood with his back to her. 'I wouldn't count on that,' he said softly.

She laughed. 'Oh, I'm not. What I'm counting on is a hot meal and a hot bath. Or a hot bath and a hot meal—I haven't decided in what order I want them yet.'

He stuffed his hands into his rear trouser pockets. 'Well, you'll have plenty of time to decide. We've at least another day's journey before we reach Kadar.'

'What?' Dorian scrambled to her knees. 'But you said——'

'I said the city was on the other side of the mountain—and it is, more or less.'

'Dammit, Jake, why did you lie to me?'

'I didn't lie,' he said mildly. 'I just thought it best not to let you worry about the distance we had to cover.'

'Then what *is* on the other side of the mountain? You said there was a town...'

'There is. It's called Quarem.'

'The place where they have the bridal market?'

Jake nodded. 'It's a rough place. I'd skirt it altogether, if I were alone. But I can't ask you to go without food much longer, and we'll need horses to get through the valley.'

'The valley?' She stared at him in bewilderment. 'What valley?'

'The valley of the Two Suns. Crossing it will take us a day and a half or so, and then we'll be in Kadar. There will be some risks, but they should be minimal, assuming you can remember your instructions.'

Dorian stared at him. Their brief truce was ending; she could hear that clipped, authoritative tone seeping back into his voice as he spoke.

'What instructions?' she asked warily.

Jake turned to her. 'You have an amazingly short memory for a reporter,' he said softly. 'Have you forgotten that you're my adoring, mute little wife?'

Her face coloured. She was his woman. No. Of course she hadn't forgotten, not after what had happened this morning.

But he never had explained why it would be necessary to keep up the farce once they were safely inside Barovnia.

'You're to defer to me at all times,' he said, bending and picking up the supply sack. He looked at her as he slung it over his shoulder. 'Keep the scarf low on your forehead. We'll do something about the way you're dressed. No respectable man would let his wife be seen in such mud-spattered, torn clothing. Just remember not to talk, not to lift your eyes unless I tell you to, and——'

'And not to breathe.' Dorian rose and faced him, her hands on her hips. 'Listen, Jake, I am not going to be led into that town like a—a donkey unless you do some explaining.'

He glowered at her. 'Haven't you been listening? You will do exactly as you are told.'

'I most certainly will not.'

'Listen to me. There are things you don't understand.'

'Then explain them.'

His face turned cold. 'They're none of your business.'

'Well, then, I'll tell you what. When we get into town, you go your way and I'll go mine. I'll find a telephone and——'

'No!' His voice was razor-sharp. 'No,' he repeated. 'You will not do that.'

Dorian's chin jutted forward. 'Give me one good reason why I shouldn't.'

Jake drew in his breath. 'Dorian, I need—I need time...'

'For what?' she said impatiently. 'For God's sake, there *is* no time. You should know that even better than I do. Jack Alexander is probably going to become the tin god in this little part of the world, and——'

His eyes narrowed. 'Is that what you think he'll be?'

'More or less. What would you say?'

Jake blew out his breath. 'I'd say the man's been asked to assume an out-of-date responsibility no one in his right mind would want.'

She looked at him, surprised by the impassioned words. 'Surely that's not Jack Alexander's opinion?'

'Of course it's his opinion,' he growled. 'He doesn't belong here.'

'Then why has he come?'

'What do you mean, why? He's come because he has no choice.'

Dorian's eyebrows rose. 'That's ridiculous. Everyone has a choice.'

'Everyone has *responsibilities*,' Jake said, his eyes blazing into hers. 'I know it's not a popular word in today's world, but it's the truth.'

'Even so—how awful could it be for someone like Alexander to become the ruler of Barovnia? There was always the possibility——'

'Each time you cross the street, you know there's a possibility you might get hit by a car. But you don't dwell on it, do you? If you did, you'd never leave your flat.'

'Come on, Jake,' she said with a little smile, 'that's not the same thing at all. One is—well, it's a disaster that might happen, while the other——'

'Being dragged away from the life you know *is* a disaster.' Jake swept out his hand in a gesture that took in everything. 'I don't belong here, dammit! I have a life of my own.' He drew a ragged breath. 'I have freedom...'

'You?' Dorian became very still. 'You, Jake?'

Their eyes met, and a dark flush rose along his cheeks. 'I'm—I'm just putting myself in Jack's place,' he said quickly. 'I know how he feels, of course. He's told me. I mean, we grew up together, and I've always—we've always...'

Jake clamped his lips together and turned away, but it didn't matter. She didn't have to see his face to know the truth. It had been right in front of her all along, she'd even bumped against it a few times—and yet she'd ignored it.

Jake Prince and Jack Alexander were one and the same man.

The realisation was dizzying. In one instant, everything in her life had changed. It was as if a fairy godmother had suddenly stepped down from the top of Mount Cristou, waved her magic wand, and changed the meadow grasses into gold.

Dorian could hardly breathe. A byline, she thought. A column! Hell, she'd get the Pulitzer!

Her gaze went to Jake, standing rigidly ahead of her. She could write about this, too, about the reluctance of this once and future king, about his desperate wish for freedom and privacy warring with his inbred sense of responsibility.

Her eyes swept over that proud, straight back. She could see the terrible tension in him, that stiffness of muscle and spine that told her his face would have taken on that cold arrogance that could be so frightening.

But he wasn't like that. Not really. She thought of how he'd soothed away her fear yesterday. She remembered how he'd protected her against Pig Face, with a combination of wit and guts and brash determination—and she remembered, too, how he'd taken her into his arms last night when fear of the unknown had set her teeth chattering, how he'd kissed her and touched her this morning.

Had he wanted her as a woman, not as a conquest? Had he turned to her for the most basic kind of comfort, knowing that soon he would not be a man but a king, that he was about to assume a burden so awesome that she could barely imagine the weight of it?

Jake, she thought, and her heart gave a strange little lurch. Jake...

She whispered his name as she reached out and laid her hand lightly on his shoulder. His muscles were bunched, taut as steel, and suddenly nothing in the world mattered but easing away his sorrow and his loneliness.

'Jake,' she said again, 'please. Don't turn away from me. Talk to me. Tell me how——'

His breath rasped as he spun around and grabbed hold of her.

'God, but you're good,' he said hoarsely. 'It's an art, you know, making someone believe you're concerned when actually you're busy composing a story inside that beautiful head.'

'No! I wasn't doing that. I wasn't even thinking of——'

'Come on.' His smile was cold and hard. 'We both know the truth. You've been after the intimate details about Alexander from the start. If only you hadn't followed me off that charter plane...'

'What's that got to do with anything? I still don't know why you were flying off into nowhere.'

'No. You don't.' His grasp tightened, until she could feel the press of each finger through her blouse. 'What went wrong this morning, Dorian, hmm?' His mouth twisted. 'Did you lose your courage at the last minute? Hell, I'll bet you've done your best investigations in the sack.'

'You—you bastard! You—you——'

'Out of words again, sweetheart?' Jake's eyes turned black. 'Just be sure you're out of them when we get to Quarem.'

Her heart seemed to shrivel within her breast. The anguish and concern she'd felt minutes ago hardened to ice.

'Don't threaten me, Jake.'

'There are a thousand things that could happen to you between here and Kadar.'

'Such melodrama,' she said, trying not to let him hear the fear in her voice. 'Don't you think you're overdoing it a bit?'

'There are tribes in my country that still deal in stolen women, Dorian. I'll bet you didn't know that.' His smile slashed across his face. 'Harems have been outlawed for years, but they still exist. And blondes always sell well.'

'Stop this.' Her voice quavered a little; she hated herself for it, and for the sly smile it brought to Jake's face.

'And then there's the bridal market at Quarem.' She tried twisting away as his hand came up to her hair; he caught some pale golden strands in his fingers and rubbed them together, as if they were silk. 'You'd bring a good price there—even if I had to have your tongue taken out first.'

Oh, God! She was trapped, trapped in a place that knew nothing of freedom, the captive of the next *abdhan* of Barovnia, a man who held the power of life and death—a man who was ruthless enough to use that power.

'You can't get away with this, Jake,' she said breathlessly. 'I know women don't have equal status in your world, but——'

She cried out as his hand swept over her, moving possessively over her hips, her buttocks, sweeping up the curve of her waist until it reached her breast.

'You're wrong.' His voice was dispassionate; it was as if he were talking about the worth of a horse or a favourite hunting dog. 'Women are very important. They're property—valuable property.' His hand cupped her breast, his thumb brushing lightly across her nipple. '*You* are property,' he said coldly, as his other hand pressed against the base of her spine and brought her closer to him. 'And you belong to me, for as long I want you.'

'When I'm free—when I get to Kadar, I'll tell the world about you,' she said hoarsely. 'I'll tell them everything, Jake. Everything!'

He laughed. 'Tell them whatever you damned please.' She struggled as he gathered her to him, but his strength overpowered her. His mouth dropped to hers; she felt the coolness of his lips, the brush of his tongue—and somewhere deep within her, in the marrow of her bones or the pulse of her blood, some dark passion uncoiled and sent heat licking through her body.

She swayed in his arms and Jake made a ragged sound in his throat as he gathered her to him, holding her so tightly that she could feel the race of their hearts intermingling.

For a moment, they were alone in the world.

And then Jake lifted his head. He clasped her shoulders and put her from him. Dorian's eyes opened slowly and met his; for one instant, she thought she saw her own confusion mirrored there, but then a harsh smile curled across his mouth and he stepped back.

'Tell them whatever you want,' he said softly. 'Don't leave anything out.'

He turned and stalked away while she stood trembling, her arms wrapped around herself for comfort. Halfway up the trail he swung around and faced her.

'Get that scarf up,' he said.

Dorian didn't move. After a moment, Jake put his hands on his hips.

'Well? Are you coming—or do I leave you for the vultures?'

When she stood her ground, he shrugged, turned his back to her, and started walking. Within seconds, he'd disappeared from sight.

High overhead, as if on cue, a wild cry rent the silence. Dorian looked up at the dark shapes soaring on the wind.

Tears of rage and frustration rose in her eyes.

'Damn you, Jake Prince,' she said softly.

Her whispered words rose like smoke into the air. After a moment, she drew the scarf over her head and set off after him.

CHAPTER NINE

THE pass merged with a dusty, unpaved road at the base of the mountain. Jake was waiting for Dorian as she skidded down the last steep section. He caught her in his arms, but there was nothing welcoming in his embrace.

'No more lagging behind,' he snapped. 'From now on, I want to know where you are at all times.'

'Is that so?' she said coldly.

'And I don't want to hear a word out of you. Have you got that?'

Dorian wrenched free of him. 'Come off it, Jake. The macho act gets tiresome after a while.'

'Behave yourself,' he said in a soft, ominous tone.

'Or?'

'Or you might just turn our little adventure into something you'll never forget.'

'You're very good at making threats. Let's just see how good you are at keeping promises—like the one you made me about getting us to Kadar.'

Jake smiled grimly. 'Just do as you're told and everything will be fine.'

He didn't know how right he was, she thought as he clasped her elbow and tugged her unceremoniously into place beside him. Everything *would* be fine—just as soon as she notified *WorldWeek* that she was coming in with the story of the decade. Walt had wanted her to find a way to wangle an interview with the next *abdhan*. What he'd meant was, get this story even if you have to go to bed with the guy, and she'd told him where he could shove that idea.

Dorian smiled. In the end, what she'd done was a lot more creative.

She'd trotted across half of forever with the publicity-shy Jake Prince or Jack Alexander or whatever in hell he wanted to call himself, learning more about him in two days than others had in years of trying.

No other reporter's story would be able to hold a candle to hers. She would get the full treatment when the news of her exclusive broke, but she didn't want it to happen in Kadar. She wanted it the minute they came trudging through the Valley of the Two Suns. She could see it now: TV cameras. Radios, microphones—she wanted it all.

And she knew exactly how to set it up. All she needed was two minutes alone with a telephone, once they reached Quarem.

Jake glanced at her. 'Keep that scarf up.'

'I thought you said there were blondes in Barovnia.'

'What did I tell you about giving me a hard time?'

'Forgive me, my lord,' Dorian said pleasantly, and she pulled the shawl high up on her head.

He gave her a glowering look. 'That's better.'

Of course it was, she thought gleefully. It was perfect! Not her ridiculous compliance: if he thought she'd believed all that stuff about the horrors that awaited her in Quarem, he was crazy.

No. What was perfect was the story she was bringing with her—and the fact that Jake, in his pitiful male arrogance, still thought she had no idea that he was the *abdhan*.

Did he really think she was that simple-minded? Was she supposed to accept the explanation that he'd been talking about his buddy, Jack Alexander, and not about himself when he'd said all those things about why he didn't want to be *abdhan*?

And the things he'd said... Dorian rolled her eyes. She'd almost fallen for that touching little speech he'd made—all that stuff about freedom and responsibility. But once she'd been marching down the trail after him again, all the loose ends had begun to knit together.

Jake had not been flying *to* Barovnia aboard that private little jet. He'd been *fleeing* from it, in a last-minute panic.

It was so obvious, once she thought about it. He had never wanted to give up his easy Western lifestyle for the rigours of being *abdhan*, but somehow the Dark Suits had talked him into it. And then, midway to Kadar, he'd balked.

'Land this plane,' he'd demanded, or something like it, 'and have a small jet fuelled and waiting for me.'

And the Dark Suits had done it. Of course they had! Who among them would have dared argue with the next *abdhan*—the *abdhazim*—even if he was trying to refuse the throne?

Jake's voice intruded on her thoughts. 'Quarem is just ahead,' he said. 'You are mute, Dorian, remember?' When she said nothing, he cursed softly. 'Dammit, do you hear me?'

'I can't speak if I'm mute,' she said sweetly.

He caught her by the shoulder and spun her towards him. Her pulse thudded when she saw the dark fire in his eyes. This trip wasn't over yet; she had to be careful not to push him too far.

'Well, it's the truth, isn't it? You have to make up your mind, Jake, if you want me to speak or not.'

A muscle bunched in his jaw. 'You're to answer me if I ask you a question,' he said finally. 'Just keep your voice down and that scarf over your mouth, and no one will know the difference.'

She nodded and they began walking again. Oh, yes, she thought, it was easy to see why the Dark Suits would have felt cowed by Jake Prince. And it was a cinch to figure out why they'd looked so unhappy as he talked to them on that runway in the middle of nowhere.

'I'm leaving,' he'd said, and there they were with a planeload of reporters and no Crown Prince. Heaven only knew what story they'd fabricated to explain his disappearing act. They were probably stonewalling it like champions.

As for Jake's rage at finding her on his heels—well, it was one thing to do a disappearing act, but having a journalist peer over your shoulder when you were doing it guaranteed notoriety. Just what a man who loathed personal publicity would want, she thought wryly.

Because of her, he'd had to rewrite his script. And it wasn't finished yet. That was why he was determined to travel incognito. Who knew what story the Dark Suits had come up with? Jake would have to contact them just to make sure their stories coincided, which meant that he'd have to use the telephone once they reached Quarem.

Well, that was right down her alley. Let him phone Kadar as fast as his fingers would dial. When he was done, she would call Walt. And then——

Jake's hand closed around her wrist. 'We're coming into the town.'

She looked up and her stomach did a funny lurch. She had expected—what? Houses. Roads. Something not terribly modern, but recognisably Western.

But Quarem didn't meet that description. It looked, she thought, exactly as a town in Eastern Europe might have looked five hundred years before. Half-timbered houses lined narrow, dusty streets. The men she could see were dark and rough-looking, and the women had an air about them. They looked worn, almost defeated.

The realisation made her feel frightened—and rebellious.

'Remember,' Jake said, 'no talking, except to me.'

'Oh, yes, master. I understand.'

'Keep that shawl over your head.'

'Certainly, sir. Is there anything else, sir?'

Jake cursed softly and pulled her against him. 'Yes. Remember to keep a civil tongue when you speak to me.'

'Or what?' She glared at him. 'Will you sell me at the bridal market?'

His smile chilled her. 'Don't be stupid. You'd bring a lot more money from the Tagor.'

She laughed. 'You're getting desperate, Jake. The Tagor, indeed! You're making all this up!'

'Behave yourself,' he said softly, 'or you just might get to meet him.'

Dorian grimaced. Who was he kidding? No matter how backward Barovnia might be, slaves, bridal markets, and bandit kings just didn't exist any more. Still, it was hard not to feel a growing sense of unease as he led her deeper into Quarem. Close up, it looked even more un-civilised and menacing—like Jake.

Two days of travelling on foot through rough terrain had honed his appearance to a menacing edge. Dark stubble covered his cheeks and chin, and dust covered his once-shiny boots. He looked like a man who had squared off against trouble more than once and had yet to find out what it was to lose. And yet—and yet she had to admit that none of that detracted from his good looks. If anything, it only emphasised them.

He was sexy and dangerous-looking, and it was a powerful combination. That was probably why she'd made such an ass of herself this morning. Jake, the bastard, had surely counted on it. How better to control a woman than to kiss her into submission? And how better to make a journalist forget her objectivity than to make her your lover?

But it would not happen again. Two more days, Jake had said, and then they'd reach Kadar. And when they did...

His arm slipped around her waist. 'Stay close to me,' he murmured.

She blinked, then caught her breath. They had reached the centre of Quarem, and, despite what she'd already seen, the reality of the market itself was staggering.

The square was cobblestoned and thronged with people and animals. Staked-out pigs and sheep competed for space with wooden cages of squawking chickens and ducks. Smells filled the air, cardamom and cinnamon and coffee mixed with the muskier tones of goat and horse. And the noise, the overwhelming cacophony of voices haggling in a language she'd never heard before...

Jake seemed to sense her confusion. He slipped his arm lightly around her shoulders.

'It's all right,' he said softly.

'My God,' she whispered. 'It's so—so——'

'Different? Yes. But I warned you it would be.' He drew her closer and she let him. 'Just keep moving. That's it. We want to look as if we belong here, remember?'

She nodded as she walked along beside him, her eyes taking in everything she saw: women, some in Western dresses years out of fashion, others dressed as she was, and some few bundled head to toe in shapeless jellabas; men, dark-eyed and fierce, most of them looking as if they'd just laid down their weapons to come into town...

But no telephones. Not that she could see, at any rate.

'Jake? Isn't there a phone?'

She felt him stiffen beside her. 'So you can contact your magazine?'

'So we can let people know we're all right.'

He shook his head. 'I'm sorry to disappoint you, Dorian, but there's no phone here.'

None for her, at any rate, she thought grimly. But surely Jake would find a way to contact the Dark Suits and warn them, not just that he was still alive, but that he was en route with a journalist in tow.

Well, two could play that game. If he found a phone, so would she. And, when she did...

'What we need is food. And horses. Then we'll take care of getting you a change of clothing.'

She looked at him as if he were crazy. 'With what? We have no money.'

'I have a pocketful of *czelnys*—more than enough to buy what we need. Just stay close to me.'

Stay close to him? She almost laughed. What else would she do? she thought as they went from stall to stall while Jake purchased provisions for the trip through the Valley of the Two Suns. She still wanted to find a telephone, but she wasn't about to dash off on her own to do it, now that she'd seen Quarem. The place was— it was alien. And—and...

A whisper of alarm danced along her skin. Someone was watching them. She looked up carefully. A huge man with a beard and turban was looking at her from across the narrow street.

She bowed her head quickly and drew her scarf closer around her. It had slipped a little, and she wondered if he'd seen the paleness of her skin or the colour of her hair. There'd been something in the way he'd looked at her...

When she looked up again, he was gone. Dorian let out a sigh of relief.

'Dorian?' Jake's voice was low. 'What's wrong?'

'Nothing,' she said quickly. 'Are we—are you almost finished?'

He nodded towards the next stall. 'We're just going to stop here to buy a change of clothing.'

The sense that she was being watched returned. Her gaze flew beyond Jake—and there was the bearded man! Dorian clutched at Jake's arm.

'Please—can't we leave now?'

His mouth tilted at the corners. 'I'm touched at your eagerness to be alone with me, kitten,' he said drily, 'but surely you can survive another few minutes in the company of my countrymen.'

'It's not that. It's—there's...' Her voice faded away. The man had vanished again.

'Look, I haven't time to play games. If there's something you want to say, say it.'

She stared at him while her brain shrieked at her to tell him about the bearded man. But what, exactly, was there to say? That she'd seen the same face a couple of times and panicked?

'Well?' he said, his voice rough with impatience.

Dorian swallowed drily. 'I—I was only going to say that I'm tired.'

Jake's brows drew together as he looked at her. His gaze moved over her face, lingering on her shadowed eyes and trembling mouth, and she waited for him to say something scathing. Instead, to her surprise, he sighed and pulled her into the curve of his shoulder.

'I know. But the next part of our journey will be easier, I promise.'

She closed her eyes for an instant as she let herself lean into him. How could it still feel so right to let him hold her close?

'I hope so,' she mumbled into his jacket. 'I've about had it with camping out under the stars.'

Jake laughed softly. 'OK. Tell you what. You stay here while I buy the horses. How does that sound?'

As if he was heading for a telephone, she thought breathlessly. She drew back and gave him what she prayed was an innocent smile.

'It sounds—it sounds like a good idea.'

His eyes narrowed. 'I assume you're not foolish enough to even think about taking off without me.'

'In a crowd like this?' She shuddered delicately. 'Believe me, Jake, I won't move an inch.'

Except to dog your footsteps... And what harm could come to her if she did that? He was going for a phone, she was certain of it.

'And you're not afraid to be alone for a few minutes?'

But she wouldn't be alone, not the way he meant. Not if she followed after him...

'Dorian?'

She shook her head. 'No. Of course not. I'll—I'll be grateful for the chance to rest.'

He gave her a long, assessing look, and then he nodded. 'All right. I won't be long, I promise.' Clasping her arm, he drew her to a stall where the counters overflowed with woollen and cotton clothing. She watched while he spoke to the heavy-set proprietor and pressed several coins into her hand. The woman peered past him at Dorian and nodded.

'OK,' Jake said when he turned back to her, 'it's all taken care of. I've explained that you're from a distant hill country. I told her that you don't understand our language and that you have an unfortunate handicap that keeps you from speaking normally, even in your own tongue.'

Dorian grimaced. 'What a charming description. What does she think of me?'

'She thinks you are a woman who needs looking after.'

'I'll bet!'

'I told her that I'm concerned for your welfare in this village of scoundrels. She promises she will take good care of you while you choose trousers and a shirt for me and a jellaba for yourself, and that she will see to it you don't wander off and get yourself into trouble.' He laughed softly as he bent and kissed her cheek. 'Get that look of outrage off your face, my beloved wife,' he whispered, 'or I'll trot you down to the marriage broker.'

Dorian gritted her teeth as Jake strolled away. Go on, she thought, enjoy yourself. I'm the one who's going to have the last laugh once we reach Kadar. In fact, once I've made this call...

The vendor caught her hand as she started to step out after Jake.

'*Bobska? Bobska, nasht vadai.*'

Dorian looked at her helplessly. The woman was taking her responsibilities seriously, dammit! Jake was almost at the end of the street; soon, he'd fade from view.

She shook her head urgently and pointed after him. But the woman only smiled gently without relinquishing her grasp in the slightest.

'*Nasht vadai.*'

'Stay here,' she was saying.

Dorian rose on tiptoe. Jake was at the corner, he was turning it...

'Dammit!' The word exploded from her lips. She swung towards the woman. 'You must let go of me. Let go, do you hear?'

The dark, liquid eyes widened. 'You—you English, *bobska*?'

'No. Not English, I'm American. I...' Dorian caught her breath. 'You—you speak my language,' she whispered.

The woman nodded. 'My *menya*—my cousin,' she said proudly. 'In Chicago.'

'Listen to me.' Dorian looked around, then moved closer. 'Do you have a phone? A phone,' she repeated sharply when the woman looked blank. 'You know. Hello? How are you? A phone!'

'Your man say you no speak, *bobska*.'

'He's not my man.' Dorian's jaw shot forward. 'He—he's taken me from my people.'

'Ahh.' The woman frowned. 'Bad, take womans.'

'Yes. And I must contact them and tell them what he's done. A phone.' She mimed putting a receiver to her ear. 'Do you have one?'

The woman shook her head. 'Office,' she said, pointing down the street. 'Tele—tele...'

'There's a telegram office in Quarem?' The woman nodded and Dorian smiled in triumph. So. That was where Jake had gone. She had been right; two could, indeed, play at this game. 'Do you have pencil and paper? Pencil and paper,' she repeated, miming writing on the palm of her hand with her finger.

The woman frowned. 'No-o...' Her eyes lit. 'Wait,' she said, and she turned and moved quickly along the narrow aisle. She was back in seconds, clutching a soiled paper sack and a tiny pencil stub. 'Pencil, paper,' she said proudly.

Dorian printed *WorldWeek's* address, then hesitated. What message could she send Walt that would tell him everything but have no meaning for anyone else? A smile curved across her mouth. She bent over the paper as the shawl slipped from her head to her shoulders.

'Assignment completed,' she wrote. 'Emperor of World in pocket. Arrive two days, Valley of Two Suns.' She signed it, 'Blondie.'

'Can you send this for me?' she said urgently. 'I—I have no money. But I'll pay you back after—after my family comes for me.'

'I do.' The woman's mouth narrowed. 'Bad man, take womans.'

Dorian nodded. 'He—the man with me—mustn't know.'

The woman nodded, too, as she took the note and stuffed it into her pocket. '*Bobska* take,' she said, pointing to the garments on the shelves.

Dorian nodded. 'Bless you,' she said breathlessly, 'you're right. This, then,' she said, pointing to a dark blue caftan. 'And—and this. And...'

The hair rose on the nape of her neck. She straightened slowly, and as she did she saw the other woman's eyes widen.

'*Vostaritch*,' she muttered, nodding her head surreptitiously at something behind Dorian.

From the look on her face, whatever she saw was not good. Dorian took a deep breath, then swung around.

Her throat constricted. It was the bearded man, only now he was on horseback. And he was not alone—two others, as big and as ugly as he, rode with him. He smiled, showing a mouthful of discoloured teeth, and said something that made the men with him burst into laughter.

'*Bobska*!' The woman from the stall shoved her, hard. 'Go,' she said urgently. 'Go, *bobska*!'

Dorian didn't hesitate. She spun away and raced blindly down the narrow street, driven by a terror so primal that it drove all rational thought out of her head. All she knew was that she had to reach Jake before the hoofbeats and that awful male laughter caught up with her.

A small herd of horses was staked just ahead, but would she find Jake there? If he'd gone to send a telegram, then she'd have to face whatever rode behind her alone.

There was no time to think about it. She ran towards the horses. It was her only chance. Jake had to be here. He *had* to be...

'Dorian?'

She fell into his outstretched arms, sobbing his name, burrowing into his embrace while she gasped for breath.

'Dorian.' His voice was rough with concern. 'Kitten, what is it?'

A tremor went through her. 'A man,' she huffed. 'A horrible man. He—he was watching me.'

'Where?' Jake grasped her shoulders and held her from him. 'Dorian. Tell me where you saw him!'

'Everywhere! And now—now he's got other men with him...'

Her words tumbled to a halt as Jake stared past her. She watched as his face changed. His eyes turned cold, his mouth narrowed—and she knew. Oh, God, she knew...

'Get behind me,' he said softly.

'Jake. Jake—who is he?'

'Dammit, woman, did you hear what I said? Get behind me. Now!'

She did, then stood trembling as she peered over his shoulder. There they were—the bearded man and his friends—looking as evil as death as they urged their horses slowly forward.

Jake said something. She couldn't understand, but there was no mistaking the intent. His voice was harsh, angry—and protective. Instinctively, she reached out and put one shaky hand on his shoulder, and he reached up and covered her fingers with his.

One of the men pointed to them, threw his head back, and laughed.

'Go to hell, you fat son of a bitch!' Jake snarled.

The bearded man snapped out a word, and the laughter stopped. He moved forward, his horse dancing with almost obscene delicacy beneath his weight, and said something.

'No,' Jake said. 'No, goddamn you!' He added something in Barovnian.

The man with the beard reached slowly into his waistband. Dorian cried out as he drew out a black revolver. Jake reached back and drew her into the curve of his arm.

'It's going to be all right, kitten,' he said softly.

But it wasn't. She knew that as soon as one of the men moved off, trotting to the small herd of horses. He grasped the staked-down reins of a large black stallion, jerked them free, and led the animal back to them.

'*Itsai*,' he snapped.

Jake took the reins slowly. 'I want you to do as I tell you, kitten.'

'Jake, please—what do they want?'

The bearded man stabbed his heels into his horse's flanks and moved quickly forward, snarling a command.

'They want us to go with them.'

'But where? Why? I don't——'

'We have no choice. They're armed—and they have many, many friends. We wouldn't stand a chance of a snowball in hell against them.'

Dorian began to tremble. 'What do they want?'

'*Itsai*!'

Jake snarled something in return, and then he leaped on to the back of the stallion and held his hand out to Dorian.

'Come,' he said softly.

She put her hand in his and scrambled up ahead of him. His arms closed around her as the other horsemen surrounded them, and the little party began moving out of Quarem.

'Jake?' Dorian swallowed hard. 'Please, you have to tell me what they want.'

He took a deep breath. 'Remember what I told you about the bridal market, kitten?'

'I thought—I thought you were joking about that.'

'No,' he said grimly. 'I was never more serious.'

'Does he think you brought me to sell? Well, tell him you didn't. Tell him——'

'I did.' His arms tightened around her. 'But he doesn't believe me. He's taking us to his leader.'

'But why? What does his leader have to do with anything?'

'*Itsai! Itsai!*'

The man riding alongside reached out and slapped his hand on the stallion's flank. The horses broke into a swift gallop, and Jake drew Dorian more closely into his arms.

'Their leader is the Tagor,' he said.

Hysterical laughter rose in her throat. There it was again, that ridiculous name. But Jake—Jake wasn't smiling, she thought as she tilted her head back and looked at him. He was cold-eyed, narrow-lipped—he looked—he looked . . .

'Jake?' Dorian drew in her breath. 'Why are they taking me to him?'

Jake's arms tightened around her. 'I won't let anything happen to you,' he said in a harsh whisper.

She felt very cold suddenly. 'Please, tell me the truth. Why is the man with the beard taking me to the—the Tagor?'

He put his mouth to her ear before he spoke, so that his whisper seemed to travel into her very bones.

'He wants to give you to him as a gift.'

Dorian waited. She waited for the punch-line to the joke, she waited for Jake to say he'd only been teasing; she waited for some terribly clever rejoinder to come dancing into her head.

But all that happened was that her heart began beating faster and faster, as if it were trying to keep time with the stallion's thudding hoofbeats, and finally the only thing that seemed to make any sense at all was to bury her face in Jake's neck and cling to him for her very life as they galloped wildly across the alien landscape.

CHAPTER TEN

DORIAN had once interviewed a young woman who'd been unfortunate enough to have been held hostage for more than twelve hours by a bank robber who'd locked her in a lavatory while he negotiated with the police.

'You must have been terrified,' Dorian had said.

The woman had nodded. 'Oh, yes, I was. It was the worst experience of my life.'

'But how did you get through it? What did you do to make the time pass?' Dorian had asked, and the woman had got a defensive look on her face.

'Well,' she'd said after a pause, 'once I realised there was nothing much I could do to change things, I slept.'

Dorian had been incredulous. The woman slept? Slept through those terrifying hours? No, she'd thought firmly, that was impossible.

Now, as they rode slowly towards the mountain encampment of the Tagor, she wondered if perhaps the woman had taken the only reasonable action.

Her mind was doing dreadful things, conjuring up scenarios that might take place once their captors turned them over to the Tagor. The imaginative scenes were vivid, frightening, and all shared an ending that was filled with violence and degradation.

Jake felt her move restlessly in his arms, and he drew her back against him.

'We'll be all right,' he whispered, his breath stirring the damp tendrils of hair on her cheek.

For some reason she didn't understand, the tender reassurances in his voice brought a lump to her throat. She wanted to fling her arms around his neck and beg him to hold her to his heart, not because of what might lie ahead, but because being close to him suddenly seemed all that mattered. All she could concentrate on now was the solace of Jake's embrace, the steady beat of his heart beneath her ear, the coolness of his lips as he brushed them against her temple.

'Close your eyes and get some rest,' he said softly as the horses picked their way through a rock-strewn valley.

She protested that sleep was impossible. But little by little fear and fatigue worked against her, until finally her head fell back against his shoulder and her eyelids drooped shut.

'That's my girl,' Jake whispered. She felt the soft press of his mouth against her hair. She thought of the woman hostage she'd interviewed, and then, mercifully, she drifted off into nothingness.

She came awake with dizzying swiftness, awakening not in a sweet, sensual haze as she had that morning, but to a formless terror, a sudden nightmare of such awful proportions that it made her gasp and jerk upright.

'Jake?' she said, and instantly his arms tightened around her.

'Easy, kitten. I'm right here.'

A tremor went through her. 'I—I was dreaming,' she whispered. Images flashed through her mind and she buried her face in his shirt. 'It was awful.'

'Trust me, Dorian. Everything will be all right.'

She nodded and waited for her heartbeat to slow. Everything would be all right, Jake had said, but she wondered if that could possibly be true. Her dream had been ugly, but reality was little better.

She sat up and looked around. The horses were moving in a line through a rocky defile, with the black stallion in the centre of the little procession. It was late afternoon: the sun was low in the sky.

'Jake? Will we be there soon?'

It was a child's question, but Jake understood the despair behind it. He nodded as he drew her back against him.

'Yes. I think so.'

Dorian hesitated. 'What—what will happen to us?'

She felt him draw a deep breath. 'I suspect we'll be cleaned up a bit and then taken to see the Tagor.'

She smiled for the first time. 'Cleaned up a bit? What for? I mean, judging by the way our escorts look and smell, soap and water isn't a priority item around here.'

'I know. But the Tagor prides himself on his civility and sophistication.'

She tilted her face up questioningly. 'You sound as if you know him.'

'No. We've never come face to face. But I've heard of him.' He gave her a tight smile. 'He's rather well-known in this part of the world.'

'Well,' she said, trying desperately for a light touch, 'he can't be very sophisticated if he believes in stealing women.'

There was nothing light in Jake's reply.

'He'd never dream of stealing you, kitten,' he said grimly. 'But accepting you as a gift from his men—well, that's different.'

Bitter-sweet laughter rose in her throat. 'I see,' she said. 'The Barovnian version of Emily Post, right? Lesson One: Never look a gift horse in the mouth.'

Jake blew out his breath. 'I guess you could put it that way.'

'But he won't really—I mean, surely not even in Barovnia ...' She hesitated. 'I suppose I shouldn't keep saying things like that. I know that we're talking about a bandit here, not a typical Barovnian.'

'There's no reason to pick your words now,' Jake said gruffly, 'not when we've just been kidnapped so you can be presented to the Tagor like a Christmas present.' He laughed bitterly. 'Hell, who have I been kidding? My country has one foot planted so firmly in the past that it will take everything short of dynamite to blast it loose.'

'Yes, but——'

'And I've always known it. It's just that I'm uncomfortable admitting it, even to myself.'

'I understand.'

Jake sighed. 'No,' he said after a pause, 'no, kitten, you don't.'

I do, though, she thought. I know who you are, Jake, I know that it wasn't selfishness or cowardice that sent you fleeing your duty—it was desperation. I know how torn you've been by the decision you had to make...

'Then explain it to me,' she said softly.

A bitter smile flashed across his face. 'Why? So you can write an exposé about the doubts of—of one of Jack Alexander's advisers?'

For a moment it was hard to think why he would think that. *WorldWeek*, and the articles she'd been sent to write, were the last things in her mind.

In the real world, the one that lay beyond these mountains, she would have given him a clever answer, one that would have made him smile even while it established the adversative relationship of reporter and subject.

But this wasn't the real world; it was a place where life had suddenly taken on special meaning, and there was no room for anything but the truth.

'No,' Dorian said softly. 'I—I just—I just want to know about you, Jake.'

His eyes darkened. 'Kitten...'

'*Javai!*'

The sharp command caught them both by surprise. The little column was coming to a halt; they had entered a broad meadow pocked with canvas tents and grazing horses.

'*Javai!*'

The behemoth was standing beside the stallion, glaring up at Dorian with his massive arms outstretched. She couldn't understand his words, but his message was precise and clear.

'Get off,' he was saying. 'Get off and I'll catch you.'

Jake slipped from the saddle before she could move and said something sharp and authoritative. Dorian held her breath while the two men stared at each other. Then, with an unpleasant laugh, the bandit waved his meaty hand in the air and stepped back.

She felt her heart begin to beat again as Jake looked up and held out his arms. She dropped into them without hesitation.

'Jake,' she whispered feverishly, 'I beg you, don't do anything that foolish again. I'd have survived——'

'But I wouldn't.' His voice was raw. 'If that son of a bitch so much as touches you—if anyone touches you——'

He fell silent, but not before the same electric message flashed between them again.

'*Sinza*!'

The giant stepped forward and so did Jake, but before either man could make a move a woman covered head to toe in a black jellaba pushed between them, barked something as she clamped a hand around Dorian's wrist, and began tugging her towards a nearby tent.

'Wait a minute,' Dorian said quickly. 'Hey! Did you hear what I said? Just wait a——'

Jake shoved past his guard. 'Go with her, kitten,' he said quietly. 'She's only going to give you a chance to eat something and get cleaned up.'

Her lip trembled. 'But—but where will you be?'

'In another tent, doing the same thing.' He touched his hand to her cheek and she fought back the desire to bury her face in his warm flesh and sob out her fear. 'Hey,' he said with a little smile, 'just this morning, you couldn't decide if it was a bath or a meal you wanted most. Now, our host is about to provide both. Besides, a little soap and water and some food will help you regain your strength.'

She looked past him to the sullen-faced men who had gathered to watch the show, to the swaddled women scattered among them, and to the tents that stood like huddled animals against the overhanging mountains. Her gaze returned to Jake, standing close beside her, and suddenly she knew that she could find all the strength she would ever need deep in his dark eyes.

She would be as brave as he was, she thought, and she lifted her head proudly and smiled back at him.

'Don't forget to wash behind your ears,' she said, and then she turned and followed her jellaba-draped guard to the tent.

Some food, Jake had said, and a little soap and water, but this interlude was not going to be that simple. Her first surprise came when her escort peeled back the tent flap and shoved her inside.

The interior was surprisingly spacious and not anywhere near as barren as she'd expected. A heavy fall of white gauzy fabric separated it into two rooms.

Dorian looked around slowly. The one she was in was quite handsome. Intricate woven hangings were draped on the walls, their colours rich and bright. This was, apparently, a dining area: a pleasant scent of coffee and spices hung in the air, softly faded carpets lay underfoot, and there was a low wooden table off to the side.

The woman poked her in the back and urged her towards the table. She waited until Dorian sat, cross-legged, on the rug before it, and then she clapped her hands sharply. A girl stepped through the tent door bearing a basin of scented water, soap, and a towel.

'*Fladai*,' her guard barked.

Dorian obliged, washing her hands and face, then blotting herself dry with the towel. The woman scowled at the girl, who scampered off. The flap opened again and a troupe of girls stepped inside, their hands laden with platters, their eyes gleaming with interest as they looked at the mysterious stranger.

The food was placed before her and Dorian stared at it. She wanted to treat this meal with casual disdain. But the sight of it made her realise how hungry she really was. She devoured the warm, flat bread spread with sweet butter, the tiny meatballs, the nuts and raisins, and she drank three cups of hot, sugary coffee before she sat back and sighed with contentment.

The woman in the jellaba clapped her hands and the platters were whisked away.

'*Fladas*,' she said, motioning towards the rear of the tent.

One of the girls hurried ahead and pulled aside the heavy curtain. Dorian rose to her feet and moved forward slowly, gaping at what awaited her.

A little soap and water, Jake had said, and that was what she'd expected—a bucket of water and a bar of coarse soap. But what she found was a huge wooden tub with high, sloped sides. Steam curled from its depths, along with the faint scents of sandalwood and oil of roses.

The woman pointed to the tub. '*Fladas*,' she said irritably.

Dorian nodded. 'Yes, I agree. A *fladas* sounds like a great idea.' She gave a meaningful look at the woman and the girls. 'But I prefer my baths in private, if you don't mind, so if you'd all please get out...?'

'*Fladas*,' the woman snapped.

'Listen, I get the message. And I'm telling you, just take your little retinue and—hey. Hey!' Dorian's voice rose in indignation as the woman grabbed hold of her, but it was useless. The girls swarmed around her like bees, buzzing with laughter as they peeled off her dirty clothing, whispering with delight when they saw her fair skin. In seconds she was naked, and the woman in the jellaba pointed sternly at the tub.

Dorian tossed her head and marched towards it with as much pride as she could manage, considering the circumstances. She stepped in, then lowered herself gingerly into the hot, scented depths. Despite herself, she gave a little sigh of pleasure, leaned back, and rested her head against the rim.

Her guard slapped her hands together and the girls rushed forward and snatched Dorian's scattered clothing from the floor. The woman looked at Dorian and said something.

She smiled sweetly. 'I've no idea what you're saying, you old witch.'

The woman put her hands on her hips and stared at Dorian. A moment passed, and then her brows rose.

'*Syet*,' she commanded, putting her hand to her nose. She made a dreadful face, then pointed to the clothing. '*Octa*,' she said with disdain, and she made a sweeping gesture to the tent door.

'Throw it out, you mean?' Dorian had to laugh. 'By all means. Please do.' She sat forward quickly. 'So long as you have something else I can put on.'

As if on cue, one of the girls stepped forward, a long length of white cotton draped in her arms. The woman made a long, harsh-sounding speech, but all that mattered was the one word Dorian understood.

Jellaba. That was what the length of cotton was, and it was for her. It looked clean and soft; even the sight of it lifted her spirits. With a weary sigh, she sank back into the tub and waved her hand, mimicking the other woman's gesture.

Where was Jake now? she wondered as she washed herself with a bar of sweet-smelling soap. He'd been right about the food and the soap and water making her feel better. But—but had those same things been in store for him? She, after all, was being gift-wrapped. But Jake—

Jake could be nothing but a detriment to these men, and he'd insulted them, too, he'd challenged their power...

'The hell with this!' she said, and she rose abruptly, sending a cascade of water sloshing on to the carpet. Her guard rushed forward, waving her hands while she barked commands, but Dorian ignored her. She stepped from the tub and snatched a towel from the hands of one of the girls, who'd gone from giggling to gaping.

'I want to see Jake,' she demanded angrily as she dried herself. The woman looked at her blankly, and Dorian said something sharp and pointed as she tossed the towel aside and snatched the clean jellaba from the girl holding it. She pulled it over her head, fluffed her fingers through her wet hair, and stalked through the hanging curtain.

Her stunned guard caught up to her at the tent door. She said something and grasped Dorian's arm, but Dorian wrenched free.

'Did you hear what I said?' she demanded. 'I want Jake.' The woman looked blank, and Dorian stamped her foot. 'I don't know how to say it in your language, dammit. I want my man!'

'Do you, kitten?'

She whirled around at the sound of Jake's voice. He was standing in the open doorway, and she hesitated only a heartbeat before she flew to him and threw her arms around his neck.

The woman said something in a sharp, high voice, but Jake ignored her and gathered Dorian close.

'Oh, Jake.' Her voice quavered a little. 'I was afraid— I was afraid...' She drew back and clasped his face between her hands. 'Did they hurt you?' she whispered.

He smiled. 'Well, the razor they gave me felt as if it's been used to shave a regiment.'

Dorian smiled back at him. 'Lady Macbeth over there probably used it to shave her moustache.' Her eyes swept across his face. 'Are you really OK?'

'Yes, kitten, I'm fine. They gave me a bowl of lamb stew and a bucket of soapy water, and—why are you laughing?'

Why *was* she laughing? Considering what might await her, there was nothing remotely funny about their situation. But Jake was here, she was in his arms, and that was all that mattered . . .

'Lamb stew and a bucket of water, indeed,' she said lightly. 'I guess it pays to be the Tagor's gift.'

Jake's smile faded. 'The Tagor,' he said softly. He waited a moment, then clasped her shoulders. 'Remember what I told you about not saying a word and letting me do all the talking?'

'You mean, you want me to pretend to be mute? But all these people know I can——'

'What I mean is that you're to speak only when spoken to and take your cues from me. Can you do that?' She nodded, and he put his hand under her chin and lifted it. 'Listen to me, kitten,' he said softly. 'You mustn't underestimate this guy's intelligence, or his power. He's absolute ruler here——'

'Like the *abdhan*,' she said, her eyes on his.

Jake's mouth twisted. 'No,' he said harshly, 'not like the *abdhan* at all. The *abdhan* is trapped by his power. If he weren't—if he weren't . . .'

His mouth dropped to hers with a sudden wild hunger. Dorian's lips parted beneath his; she rose on her toes and pressed herself close to him—and suddenly a beefy hand clamped down on her arm and dragged her from Jake's arms.

The bearded behemoth glared at the two of them with fury in his eyes. He snarled a command and pointed to the door.

'OK,' Jake said softly, 'this is it, kitten. It's show time.'

It seemed a strange way to describe what lay ahead, she thought. But once they'd stepped inside the tent of the Tagor Jake's choice of words seemed to make absolute sense.

The tent was large, draped inside with billowing lengths of crimson silk that added to the sense of enormous size. The Tagor seemed even more enormous. He sat on a carved chair that stood on a elevated platform, his huge body wrapped in what looked to be yards of embroidered cloth.

Their bearded escort thrust them into the centre of the tent, bowed, then backed out of the door, leaving Jake and Dorian alone with the Tagor.

Jake glanced at Dorian. 'Get your head down,' he whispered fiercely.

'Why? You're not bowing to him. Why should——?'

She caught her breath as Jake put his hand on her head and shoved it down.

'You're female,' he said sharply.

'Well, it doesn't take brains to figure that out, Jake. If I weren't female, nobody would have bothered offering me up to him,' she muttered, eyes on the lush rugs that carpeted the floor.

'Dorian, dammit, shut up!'

The Tagor barked something at Jake.

'What's he saying?' Dorian asked.

'He says you are very beautiful.'

She sighed. 'That's only because I don't have a moustache.'

'He says, too, that you need to have some respect beaten into you.' Jake's mouth twisted. 'I told him that I agree.'

'What? Listen here, Jake...'

The Tagor spoke again and Jake laughed politely.

'What's he saying now?'

'He says he will be happy to do the job for me. He will make you into a loving, obedient woman.'

'And? What did you tell him?'

'I told him that he would need God on his side to succeed where I have not.'

Dorian's head came up sharply. 'I thought you told me everything would be all right.'

'It will be, dammit. Get your head down and shut up!'

'It *won't* be, if you play along with him.'

The Tagor growled a command. Jake caught Dorian's arm and drew her forward.

'Sit,' he said, pointing to a small, low stool before the throne.

'I don't want to sit, I want to——' She gasped as Jake shoved her on to the stool. The Tagor gave a booming laugh and motioned Jake closer.

The men entered into a long conversation. Dorian kept her head down, but every now and then she risked a quick glance from under her lashes. The Tagor kept pointing at her and Jake kept shaking his head. She could tell, from his tone and demeanour, that he was being politely but coldly firm about something.

About her, she thought with a little shiver. But—but this was ridiculous. The twenty-first century was on the horizon, and here she was, sitting like a polite lump of dough while her fate was being debated, and no one had yet asked her what she thought about it.

'Jake? Excuse me. Jake?'

Jake spun towards her, his eyes dark with barely suppressed anger.

'What is it now?' he snapped.

'I think I have the right to know what's going on. I mean, this discussion is about me, isn't it?'

'Dorian, dammit to hell, what did we agree?'

'I know,' she spat. 'I said I'd keep quiet. But you speak his language, Jake. You could translate for me. You could explain to him that—that no one does this kind of thing where I come from——'

'Listen to me. If you don't want to end up as his newest
toy, you'll look down at the floor and keep still!'

She stared at him. 'You wouldn't let that happen to
me,' she whispered. 'Would you?'

'Yes,' Jake snarled. 'I damn well would. It would be
no more than you deserved. It would...' He fell silent.
'All right,' he said grimly, 'here it is without any sugar
coating. If I can't talk my way out of this, he'll kill me
and give you to his men.'

'What? You're not serious!'

'I'm dead serious. I've explained that we're from
America——'

'Doesn't he wonder why you can speak his language?'

'I told him that I was born in this part of the world,
that you were my fiancée and I was having trouble with
you so I took you to the bridal market as a joke.'

Dorian gave the Tagor a sidelong glance. 'Some joke,'
she said shakily.

'I said I'd hoped it would scare you into behaving as
a woman should.'

'I just don't see how that's going to get us out of this,'
she said in a small voice. 'Why would that keep him
from—from...?'

'Because,' Jake said patiently, 'I've presented it all as
if it were a puzzle to solve. He's bored, Dorian. Hell,
who wouldn't be, when all you have to do is snap your
fingers to get whatever you want?'

For just a moment she forgot everything but Jake.

'Power can be exciting,' she said softly, 'it can be a
challenge.'

Jake's eyes narrowed. 'That's simplistic nonsense.'

'It isn't. If you——'

The Tagor snarled. Jake turned and listened.

'He says,' he translated, 'that he permits us this behaviour only because you are a foreigner and a barbarian. He says he allows us to behave in his presence

as we would behave in the presence of our own king so that he might learn something of our country.'

'I hope you told him that *he's* given the word ''barbarian'' a whole new meaning.'

Jake sighed wearily. 'The bottom line is that he's given us permission to stand in his presence and to look towards him. Not *at* him. Don't push our luck.'

The Tagor grunted and motioned Jake closer. After a long time, Jake inclined his head, made his way back to Dorian, and took her arm.

'Smile and curtsy.'

'Curtsy? Americans don't——'

'Just do it, dammit! That's it. Now walk with me— backwards, *backwards*! Good girl.'

She took a deep breath as they stepped outside. Night had fallen: the meadow was black, except for the blazing lights of a hundred camp-fires.

'Jake? What's going to happen now?'

As if in answer to her question, the bearded giant stepped towards them. But he didn't touch them this time; instead, he motioned them towards the tent opposite the Tagor's.

The tent's furnishings were sparse. Except for a tumble of blankets, and a hissing kerosene lamp atop a small table, it was unadorned.

Dorian turned to Jake as soon as they were inside. 'Well? What will he——?'

Jake clamped his hand over her mouth and pointed to the shadow of their guard, silhouetted on the tent door. She nodded and followed him through the tent's shadowy depths.

'Please,' she whispered, 'tell me what happens next?'

'He was very understanding, kitten. He told me he's dealt with some difficult women himself.'

She tried to laugh, although the sound she made was, despite her show of bravado, choked and false.

'What did he do, have them beheaded?'

Jake put his arms around her. 'He assured me that all such a woman needs is a Barovnian husband.'

'Yes. I can imagine.' Dorian shuddered. 'Shoeless in the winter, pregnant in the summer, and an occasional beating as a reminder of who's boss.'

Jake laughed softly and tilted her face up to his. 'I'm not sure about the shoeless thing, and the beating is ridiculous—but the rest isn't a bad idea.' He bent and kissed her, a long, sweet kiss that stole her breath away. 'Not a bad idea at all.' His hand slipped down her spine, lightly tracing her vertebrae. 'As for bringing a recalcitrant woman into line, I've always found that long, slow loving is the best method.'

Dorian shuddered beneath his touch. 'I can't—I can't think when you—when you——'

He smiled. 'Exactly. That's why the Tagor reminded me of an old Barovnian proverb: "A husband who wishes his wife to behave sees to it that she can feel but not think."'

'And—and what did you say?' she whispered.

His mouth took hers again in a kiss that grew deeper and more passionate as it went on, until finally he cupped her face in his hands and drew back, just far enough so that he could see into her eyes.

'I said that he was absolutely right,' he whispered, 'that it was clear to me that what you needed was a good Barovnian husband. We agreed that you must have one.'

Dorian's heart plummeted. 'My God,' she whispered. 'Jake, how could you? If he—if he tries to take me as his wife, if—if——'

She fell silent. Outside the tent, the sound of soft drums and flutes began rising on the cool night air.

'You've got it all wrong, kitten. The Tagor told me he thanked his men for their thoughtful gesture——'

'For me, you mean?'

He nodded. 'Yes. He hated to turn down such a gift, but he says he has far too many wives already.'

'Then—then what...?'

Jake lifted her face to his and kissed her until she was breathless.

'But he will see to it that you have a Barovnian husband,' he said softly. 'In fact, he's determined to take care of it tonight.'

She knew what he was telling her—it was in Jake's eyes, it was in the sudden leap of her blood. Still, she had to put the question to him.

'And—and who will my husband be?' she whispered.

Jake smiled, just as he had the night they'd met, when he'd asked her to go away with him and—for the swift beat of her pulse—she'd wanted to say that she would.

'Who?' she repeated.

He drew her close and kissed her deeply, and then he whispered against her lips.

'Guess.'

CHAPTER ELEVEN

HE HAD kissed her and kissed her, and he was still holding her in his arms. Maybe that was why she couldn't think coherently. Maybe that was why she'd thought he'd said—he'd said——

'This is—it's a joke, right?'

Jake smiled wryly. 'Life is full of surprises, kitten. For instance, I never dreamed I'd propose to a woman in a tent in the middle of a camp filled with bandits.'

Dorian swallowed with effort. 'Come on, Jake. You and the Tagor decided that—that you'd teach me a lesson...' She waited for him to say something, but he didn't. He just went on looking at her with that little smile curled across his mouth and a look in his eyes that she could not quite define.

'You're—you're serious,' she whispered after long seconds had crept by. 'You really told that—that awful man that we'd——'

'I didn't "tell" him anything, Dorian.'

'I don't—I don't understand.'

'The Tagor sees himself as a civilised man. That's why he's agreed to let me keep you.'

'Keep me?' she said, staring at him.

'Yes. I told you, he thinks you're my fiancée. That means I have certain rights and obligations.'

'My God! If that's his idea of civilised——'

'But he's not about to wish us *bon voyage* and send us on our way.'

Dorian swallowed drily. 'He's not?'

'The way he sees it, you're a desirable woman. All you need is some taming. If I don't exercise my rights and perform my obligations, someone else will. You get your choice, lady. Me—or one of the Tagor's men.'

152

She stared at him. 'But that's—that's crazy!'

A strange half-smile twisted across his mouth. 'Like it or not, kitten, he holds all the cards. It's either do as he says—or do as he says.'

Dorian nodded slowly. Marriage, she thought, marriage—to Jake. Not that it would be a real marriage, of course. But marriage...

The ceremony would, no doubt, be exotic and colourful, something she could write about for *WorldWeek* that would probably sell more copies of the magazine than ever before.

I Was the Bride of the Abdhan, by Dorian Oliver.

Her heart gave an unsteady lurch in her breast. Jake's bride. What a ridiculous idea...

'Well?' She looked up. Jake was watching her, and suddenly she wished the lighting was better so that she could see beyond the shadows and into his eyes. 'What's it going to be, Dorian?' He gave a little laugh. 'The barbarian you know—or the one you don't?'

'Don't say that,' she said quickly.

'Why not?' His voice was brusque. 'It's what you're thinking, isn't it?'

'Jake, for God's sake, I'm only thinking that—that getting married is—is——'

'Yeah.' The air puffed from his lungs. 'I know exactly how you feel.'

No, she thought, watching him, he didn't. How could he, when she didn't know how she felt herself?

Marriage. Marriage, to Jake...

'It's a hell of a thing,' he said as he bent over the kerosene lamp and turned up the flame, 'being forced to go through a farce like this.'

There it was again, that little constriction within her chest. But why?

'Yes,' she said slowly, 'it is, isn't it?'

'The ceremony won't be binding, of course. We won't have to bother with an annulment, in case you were concerned about that.'

'I understand.'

But she didn't. She didn't understand why she ached so, why she wanted to take a step forward and touch him.

'We can forget it ever happened, once we get out of here.' Jake turned and looked at her.

Why was he making an issue of it? She understood the situation. If they had to go through with a charade to save their necks, then that's what they'd do. And then it would be over; it would have no meaning in her life or his.

She nodded her head.

'Good,' he said gruffly. 'In the morning, when we leave—— '

'In the morning?' A little note of panic threaded through her voice. 'What do you mean, in the morning? Must we stay the night?'

'We have no choice.'

'But why? If we go through with the ceremony...'

'Use your head, Dorian. What would he think if a newly married couple denied themselves the pleasures of their wedding night?'

He smiled, and a little stab of pain twisted into her heart. This was a game to him, she thought, a game, but to her—to her...

'I know this must seem amusing to you,' she said stiffly. 'But I'm finding it anything but funny.'

'Dammit, will you listen?' His hands tightened on her and he shook her. 'If the Tagor so much as suspects that we've played him for a fool, he'll give you to one of his men—or maybe to all of them. He'll make me watch—and then, when they're finished, he'll cut out my heart. Is that blunt enough for you?'

It was blunt enough to turn her knees to water. 'Oh, God!'

Jake nodded grimly. 'Exactly. So we'll do whatever we can to convince him that we treat this marriage as seriously as he does.'

'Dammit, Jake, how do we do that?'

'We make it obvious that we're happy as hell about tonight's little shindig.'

'How? Do we laugh all the time? Do we go out there skipping? I don't understand what you expect——'

'I'll show you, then,' he said, and he pulled her into his arms and kissed her.

It took no great imagination to figure out what he was doing. His kisses were deep, almost bruising. When he was finished, her lips would be pink and swollen, her cheeks flushed. She would look like a woman eager for the marriage bed.

Jake drew back a little and looked at her. 'You're not co-operating,' he said softly.

'I don't have to,' she said a little unsteadily. 'And I don't want to...'

He gathered her closer and kissed her again, and still she stood immobile in his arms.

'Kitten,' he whispered. 'Kiss me back.' His mouth moved along her cheek, to her ear, and a tremor went through her. 'We have to be convincing, remember?' Her eyes closed as his tongue brushed the sensitive skin behind her lobe. 'How will it look if my bride is cold as stone?'

'I'm not—I'm not...' She whimpered softly as his hand swept over her, across the curve of her hip, up over her midriff, and cupped her breast.

'You see?' His voice was hoarse and low. 'It isn't so difficult to pretend to feel desire for me, kitten, is it?'

'Jake. Jake, don't...'

She groaned into his mouth as his hand slipped inside the deep neck of the jellaba. His fingers were hard and rough against her flesh; she felt her nipple leap to his touch, felt the answering leap of flame deep within her womb.

Jake's breath sighed against her skin. 'Yes, kitten. That's the way.'

Outside, in the darkness, the sound of the drums quickened, until their pulsing beat matched the race of Dorian's heart. Her hands crept up Jake's chest, to his shoulders; she moved blindly against him, and her mouth opened to his kiss.

The women came bursting into the tent, laughing as they wrenched her from his arms. The dour-faced one who had supervised her bath and her meal peered into Dorian's flushed face and clapped Jake on the back.

'She says that you look like a woman ready for her man,' he whispered as they took her from him, and Dorian knew that he was right.

They took her to the women's tent, where she stood trembling while her attendants stripped her of the jellaba and rubbed her skin with scented oil. They brushed her hair until it gleamed like pale gold, and while they fluttered around her they laughed softly and nudged each other.

Dorian had never been the kind of girl who'd spent much time thinking about marriage. She'd assumed, if pressed, that she'd fall in love some day and marry, but it had all been hazy, the kind of misty stuff that would come with the future and wasn't quite as important as the present.

But she knew what her wedding day would be like. The church would be decorated in yellow and white. Her father would give her away while her mother looked on with teary eyes; the girls she'd grown up with would be her bridesmaids, and all the people who'd ever mattered in her life would be waiting to see her come down the aisle.

Certainly, she'd never imagined a wedding like this. To be given away by the Tagor when he'd just as soon give her to any—or all—of his men, in a place of dark tents and wine-red carpets, where the guests were as likely to carve each other up as toast the happy couple, was beyond her wildest dreams.

'*Tastavai, bobska, tastavai.*'

'Turn around,' they were saying. They were saying other things, too, the kind of off-colour jokes brides-maids might make, she was certain of it. Well, at least that crossed cultural barriers. There were sexy jokes, and bridesmaids, there was a bride—and there was a groom.

'*Bobska. Vrostovia, simsaja, eh?*'

Someone handed her a pair of wispy silk underpants and she stepped into them. A bridegroom, she thought. Jake. Jake was to be her bridegroom.

'*Bobska. Tsisenjai.*' She looked up, bewildered. One of the women clucked her tongue impatiently. '*Tsisenjai,*' she said, and she grabbed Dorian's arms and lifted them over her head.

Jake. Jake. She was marrying Jake...

Her heart skipped a beat as they slipped a cotton gown over her head. Hands moved lightly across her body, smoothing the gown at her hips, then working at its rear closure. One of the women bent and placed a pair of delicate leather sandals before her, and Dorian stepped into them. At last, her attendants stood back and nodded their heads.

'*Da, bobska,*' one of them said softly.

Someone put a hand in the small of her back and pro-pelled her through the curtain to the rear of the tent. The tub was empty now, and beside it stood a standing oval mirror. Giggling, the women urged her towards it.

Suddenly, the last thing Dorian wanted was to see herself in her wedding gown. She shook her head as they pushed her forwards.

'I'm sure this is the latest in wedding finery,' she said with forced lightness, 'but it doesn't much matter to me what I look like. For all I care...'

Her eyes met her reflection in the mirror, and she fell silent.

The gown was beautiful by anyone's standards. It was made of white eyelet, with a low, off-the-shoulder neckline that emphasised the curve of her throat and

breasts. The sleeves were short and puffed, and the
bodice fitted snugly at her waist before becoming a
swirling, ankle-length skirt.

A lump rose in Dorian's throat. 'Oh,' she said softly.
'It's—it's lovely.'

One of the women stepped forward and placed a
slender wreath of pale yellow and white flowers on her
hair. She smiled and said something, and Dorian knew
she must be asking if the bride was pleased with how
she looked.

'Yes,' she murmured, 'oh, yes. I look—I look——'

To her horror, her eyes filled with tears. She looked
like a woman on her way to the arms of her beloved.
But that was a lie. What was going to happen in the next
few minutes wasn't real, it had nothing to do with love...

'*Bobska*.' The dour-faced woman leaned forward and
pressed her cheek to Dorian's. '*Oskavit*,' she said, and
Dorian could only hope that it had been a traditional
offering of good fortune.

She was going to need it.

It was quiet when she stepped from the tent, and very
bright despite the hour. Bonfires ringed the encampment, and an ivory moon hung in the sky. A
balalaika whispered a poignant song into the night, and
ahead—ahead, a carpeted path stretched towards the
brightest fire of all, where the hulking shape of the Tagor
waited.

Dorian's heart began to pound. She couldn't go
through with this, not even if it meant——

'Kitten.'

She caught her breath as Jake stepped out of the
shadows. He was smiling, and it was a different smile
from any she'd ever seen on his face before. It was tender
and welcoming, and when he put out his hand she hesitated only an instant before she took it. His fingers laced
through hers and he led her forwards through the
darkness and towards the Tagor.

She moved slowly, her sandalled feet whispering against the soft carpet, her eyes on Jake's face. No, she thought, this was not the wedding she'd imagined would someday be hers. But it *was* her wedding. Hers, and Jake's.

He had been dressed for this occasion, too, in a silky black shirt, leather vest, and close-fitting woollen trousers. His boots had been polished until the dust of the trail was not even a memory.

He looked both civilised and barbaric—he looked like the Jake Prince who'd picked her up along the road a lifetime ago and he looked like the man who would be *abdhan*. But most of all, most of all, he looked like...

Her heart thudded. He looked like the man she had fallen in love with.

No. It was out of the question. They were adversaries; they'd been that from the start and they still were. Hadn't she wired ahead and arranged to turn him into a headline? Hadn't he carefully kept his identity secret from her?

But all of that had nothing to do with the simple truth. She loved him, she loved Jake Prince or Jack Alexander or the next *abdhan* of Barovnia—she loved him in whatever guise and identity he chose, because no one part of him was indistinguishable from the others.

He was an adventurer and a man who sat behind a desk, he was a dreamer and a doer—and she loved him. And, because she did, she could not go through with this sham. It was bad enough to go through with a pretend marriage to a man who meant nothing to you, but, when you loved the man, how could you participate in such a lie and ever face yourself—or him—again?

She came to a stumbling halt just as they reached the Tagor. 'Jake,' she whispered urgently, 'I can't do this!'

'You can, kitten. You must!'

'No. Jake, no. Please——'

The Tagor spoke. Jake nodded and turned to Dorian. 'He asks if I have lied to him. He says if you have no love in your heart for me, you must tell him so now.'

Her throat constricted. 'Jake. Tell him—tell him...'

Jake cupped her face and gave her a gentle kiss. 'Don't lose your courage now,' he said softly.

His voice was as loving as his kiss. But she knew it was only meant to deceive the Tagor.

The Tagor! In her selfishness she had almost forgotten him. Her glance flew to the chieftain. He had changed his clothing for the wedding, but everything else about him was the same as she remembered, especially the stern, unyielding cast of his swarthy face.

Was she crazy? If she didn't go through with this ceremony, the Tagor would give her away like a party favour. Worse, he'd kill Jake. And a world without Jake was not a world worth living in.

'Kitten?'

Dorian looked straight at the Tagor. 'Tell him I am eager to be your wife,' she said quietly.

Jake put his arm around her waist and drew her close to his side as the Tagor spoke.

'He says that the joining of two people is not to be taken lightly,' he translated, while the chieftain's deep voice rumbled. 'He says that life is a long journey that should not be taken alone. Man and woman should undertake this journey together.' Jake paused. 'He asks if I love you.'

Dorian looked at him. 'And what did you say?' she whispered.

Jake's eyes met hers. 'I said that I love you with all my heart.'

Of course. What other answer could he have given, if they were to get out of this in one piece?

'Now he asks if you love me.'

Her mouth trembled. 'Yes. Tell him I say yes, that I will love you always.'

Jake's arm tightened around her. 'He says, then, that you are mine, and I am yours.'

She swallowed. 'You mean—it's over? We're husband and wife?'

'Yes.' He turned her to him and his hand cupped her cheek. 'We're married, kitten.'

Married. *They were married*!

A shout rose up from the assemblage, and Jake smiled. 'We're getting comments from the sidelines. They want me to kiss the bride.'

Dorian smiled, too, and blinked back the tears burning in her eyes.

'Then do it,' she said lightly.

Jake bent to her and kissed her. It was a kiss meant for the crowd, and they responded to it with good-natured laughter and a smattering of applause. Off in the distance, the balalaika began playing again, joined now by a drum and tambourine, and suddenly Jake swung her up into his arms.

'Jake? What are you doing?'

'Claiming my bride,' he whispered, and his mouth dropped to hers again.

The crowd cheered and parted for him as he strode through it, and all the while he never stopped kissing her. It was part of their performance, she knew that; she told herself that she was only doing her bit when she wound her arms around his neck and kissed him back. The charade would end once they'd left the bonfires—and the crowd—behind.

But it didn't end; it changed, instead, so that by the time they'd reached the darkness of their tent Jake was kissing her with a hungry passion. He lowered her to her feet slowly, letting her body slide down the hard length of his, and she knew without question how much he wanted her.

Not that it was a surprise: he'd wanted her from the start—he'd been honest about that.

Now they were alone, a million miles from reality.

Why wouldn't he want to play this game to its end?

She wouldn't let him, though. To let him make love to her would only make their parting more difficult. It would only make forgetting what had happened this night impossible.

That was what her head was telling her. But her body wasn't listening to her head—it was responding wildly to Jake's touch, to his taste and smell, it was warming under the soft stroke of his hand, quickening under the cleverness of his fingers.

His mouth was hot and open against hers. She made a little whimpering sound as his tongue explored hers. Slowly, inexorably, her hands lifted to his head and her fingers curled tightly into his dark hair.

Jake shuddered at her touch. 'Yes,' he whispered.

Her head fell back as he bent to her and pressed kisses against her throat. His teeth bit gently at the swelling flesh above her gown's neckline.

'I've never wanted a woman as I want you,' he whispered. He cupped her buttocks and brought her tightly against him. 'Feel what you do to me, kitten.'

She felt it: the heat, the hardness. And she wanted that, she wanted the tightly leashed power of him in her arms and in her body, she wanted...

'This is our wedding night, kitten. How can we deny what we feel on a night such as this?'

Dorian felt the sharp sting of tears. 'Our wedding night,' he'd said. But it wasn't that at all; it was only a sham. But if she let him take her, if she let him make this a night she could never forget...

'Tell me you want me as much as I want you,' he said softly.

'No. Jake, I—I can't.'

His fingers were moving down her spine; she felt the coolness of the night air on her skin.

'Jake, you mustn't. Please——'

But her whispered protest was meaningless; it hadn't the power to stand up to his kisses or his caresses. Her gown floated to her ankles like a gentle snowfall. She moaned softly as Jake's hands began moving over her.

'I can feel your desire, kitten,' he said softly. She stood, trembling, while his fingers brushed lightly across her budded nipples. 'Here,' he said, 'and here...'

She cried out as he touched the dampness of her womanhood. 'Oh, Jake. Jake, I—I can't...'

'You can.' His whispered words were fierce. 'You're my wife, kitten. You belong to me now.'

You belong to me. How barbaric those words had sounded, only a little while ago. Now—now, they sent a tremor of longing spiralling through her. If only she did belong to him. If only—if only all of this were real. If only...

A match hissed in the darkness. She blinked. Jake stood in a pool of golden candle-light, watching her.

'Ah, kitten,' he whispered, 'you're so beautiful.'

Was she? Suddenly, she wanted to be beautiful, she wanted to be everything Jake could ever desire in a woman.

He took her hand and drew her gently to him.

'Undress me,' he said softly.

Her fingers shook as she undid the first button of his shirt and then the next. Jake caught his breath as she touched his skin; he clasped her wrist, brought her hand to his lips, and pressed his mouth to her palm. His clothing fell away as hers had, until finally he stood proud and unashamed in the candle's glow.

He was beautiful, too; she wanted to tell him that. But how could she talk when his hands and mouth were searching out all her secrets? She was a creature made of crystal and air, shimmering with light and desire, and when he drew her down with him into the darkness she was trembling.

'Dorian,' he whispered. 'My wife.'

His kisses were flames burning her skin everywhere, his whispers promises of pleasures yet to come. Moaning, she moved against him, her body on fire, her hands learning the hardness of silken skin stretched taut over muscle.

When he entered her she cried out, a long, keening sigh that broke from her throat in wonder. Trembling, she called out his name and he held her close, his body shaking, too, as he fought for control.

'Slowly, kitten,' he whispered into her throat. 'We have the whole night for love.'

A night. What was one night, when she wanted forever? And they *had* forever, she thought suddenly. There were things to sort out, but Jake—Jake . . .

'Ohhh.'

Her cry rose into the darkness and was captured in Jake's kiss. I love you, she thought—and then she was beyond thought: she was adrift in the night and the darkness, guided only by the sweet, fierce power that filled her.

The tent was dark when she came awake, stirred from sleep by his caress.

'Mmm,' she sighed, her mouth pressed to his throat.

Jake kissed her. 'Sleepyhead,' he whispered as his hand moved over her, his fingers stroking lightly across her nipples. 'So you're finally awake, hmm?'

Dorian smiled. 'How could I not be?' Her breath caught as he trailed his fingers down her belly. 'It's very hard to sleep when you're—when you're doing that . . .'

'It's hard to sleep when you're in my arms, kitten,' he whispered. 'It seems a shame to waste this night.'

This night. Was he telling her that this night was all they had?

'Dorian—I don't know if you realise how different things will be, once we reach Kadar.' She heard the rasp of his breath. 'You'll be Dorian Oliver again, *WorldWeek*'s reporter on the scene——'

'*WorldWeek*?' She smiled into the darkness. 'What's that?'

Jake kissed her. 'And I—I'll be—I'll be . . .'

'You'll be the *abdhazim*.'

He went still in her arms. 'You know?'

She sighed. 'Yes.'

'When . . .?'

'I don't know, exactly. I thought that's who you were, at first, and then you convinced me otherwise. But when we were on the way to Quarem . . .'

Her breath caught. Quarem. The telegram. She had to tell him about the telegram . . .

'Dorian.' He stroked the hair back from her face. 'These last few days with you—they've meant everything to me. I never dreamed my last hours of freedom would be so sweet.'

'Your last hours . . .?'

'Yes. My advisers almost went crazy when I told them I was going to fly into Kadar alone, but——'

'Is that what you were doing? I thought—I thought you'd changed your mind about becoming *abdhan*.'

'How could I change my mind about a responsibility?' He kissed her gently. 'I just wanted the luxury of being Jack Alexander a little while longer.'

Dorian touched his cheek. 'Or Jake Prince.'

'No, love. I never expected to be lucky enough to be a man named Jake Prince—or for these days to have been so special.'

Her heart lifted at those simple words. 'Have they been?' she whispered.

He rolled to his side and took her with him, holding her close in the hard curve of his arm. There was a silence before he spoke again.

'When I was eighteen, I met a woman. I met her at a party, one of those university madhouses where there are too many people, too much noise, and too much booze. I wasn't much for that kind of thing, but I'd let my room-mate talk me into going.' He drew in his breath, then expelled it. 'I'd been having a bad time. I'd just lost both my parents in an accident——'

'At eighteen? How painful that must have been.'

'I suppose I was feeling sorry for myself, and very much adrift. I'd always had this strange division in my life because my father was a Barovnian diplomat, part of the royal family, and my mother was an American. Losing them made me feel as if I'd lost the only solid ground I had. So there I was, vulnerable as hell, and there *she* was, this woman, a little older, very beautiful—and very understanding.'

'But she hurt you, didn't she? I can hear it in your voice.'

'We became lovers. We were inseparable for a couple of weeks.' He drew his arm from under Dorian's head, sat up, and wrapped his arms around his knees. 'And I trusted her. I told her things—I talked about how hard it was to live in two different worlds, about the tragedy of the poverty that still plagued my father's birthplace...'

Dorian sat up, too. 'And?' she asked softly.

'And,' he said, his voice hardening, 'about a month after the affair ended, everything I'd said was splashed across four columns in the sleaziest of the tabloids—including some not-so-subtle references about what it was like to go to bed with—I think her phrase was "a magnificent savage" like me.'

'Oh, Jake!' Dorian put her arms around him and pressed her cheek to his back. 'It must have been horrible.'

'Yeah.' His voice was gruff. 'But it was a lesson, and I never forgot it, a lesson about reporters—and about women.'

His words drove a knife into her heart. The telegram, she thought, the telegram!

Perhaps it hadn't been sent.

'Jake—are we—are we going to Kadar through the Valley of the Two Suns?'

He turned and took her into his arms. 'Just listen to this woman,' he said, drawing her down beside him. 'She wants a geography lesson at a moment like this.'

'Jake, please—it's important.'

The old woman hadn't spoken English very well, had she? Perhaps she hadn't really understood.

'This is more important,' he whispered.

Perhaps there wasn't a telegraph office in Quarem after all. Perhaps...

Jake bent to her, and she was lost.

When she awoke next, grey light was filtering into the tent. Jake was fully dressed and leaning over her.

'I've been out scouting,' he said quietly. 'Our pals are still sleeping off the party. I want to get going before they awaken and change their minds about letting the guest of honour leave.'

She dressed quickly, then crept after him out of the tent and through the silent encampment. A herd of horses was grazing just beyond the tents. Jake held up his hand and Dorian stood still while he moved in among the animals. Minutes later, he emerged on the back of a white horse.

'Give me your hand,' he said, and he swung Dorian up behind him.

'Jake?' She put her arms around his waist and leaned close to him. 'When will we get to the Valley of the Two Suns?'

'Why do you keep asking me that?'

Because I've betrayed you, she thought. No. She hadn't, not really, she'd only been doing her job. But it was too much to explain now.

'Dorian?'

'I must talk to you,' she whispered. 'Before we reach the valley.'

Jake hesitated. 'We'll make a stop before then, OK? Now, hold on tight, kitten. We're going to ride hard.'

They rode for what seemed like hours. How could she tell Jake about what might be waiting for them? What could she say? No matter what she said, he wouldn't like hearing it, but he'd understand. He had to understand.

The mare reared wildly as a shattering roar filled the air. Dorian ducked as an enormous dark shadow swooped over them.

It was a helicopter.

'Jake,' she shouted, 'Jake, look...'

But he'd already jumped to the ground. He clasped Dorian around the waist and brought her down beside him, and then he began waving his arms over his head.

The 'copter dipped down for a closer look, then settled slowly to the ground ahead of them. The engine whined to silence as a handful of men tumbled out and trotted to where Dorian and Jake stood.

'My lord!' The tallest of the men dropped to his knees. 'Thank God you are all right!'

'Get up, Kasmir. I'm happy to see you got my message.'

'From Quarem. Yes, it reached us yesterday.' The man smiled. 'It is good that you remembered this ridge.'

'How is my cousin? Is he——?'

'He lives, my lord, but in a coma. The surgeons say we must wait.'

Jake nodded. 'Well, then,' he said briskly, 'let's get going. I'll want to see him as soon as possible.'

Dorian moved closer to Jake's side. 'You told them to meet us here?'

'Yes.'

'Then—we're not going through the valley?'

Jake's mouth twisted. 'No.'

'But you told me——'

'I know what I told you. But it made more sense to arrange to be met here.'

She nodded. 'Because—because you didn't trust me.'

He thrust his fingers through his hair. 'Dammit, Dorian, does it really matter now?'

'Yes, it does,' she said. She thought of the anguish she'd suffered, thinking he was going to walk into the trap she'd set. 'Why didn't you tell me the truth when I asked how we'd be entering Kadar?'

His mouth turned down. 'As long as we're asking questions, why did you keep asking?'

'My lord.' Kasmir stepped forward. 'I would suggest that Miss Oliver had a very special interest in your point of entry.' He looked at Dorian, his eyes as cold and flat as a serpent's. 'An army of reporters and photographers awaits you at the Valley of the Two Suns, my lord. They have been there since last night, at Miss Oliver's direction.'

Dorian shook her head as Jake swung towards her. 'No,' she said quickly, 'that's not so.'

'It is, my lord. I myself saw a copy of the wire.'

'Well, yes, I mean, I sent it.' Dorian flung out her arms as Jake stared at her. 'But—but I sent it before— before—Jake, don't look at me like that! I was going to tell you.'

'When were you going to tell me?' He caught hold of her and drew her aside. 'When the first flash bulb exploded in my face?'

'No!'

He thrust her from him as if she were something evil and poisonous. 'Keep the hell away from me,' he said in a soft, terrible whisper. 'Do you understand?'

'Jake, please, you have to listen. After—after last night...' Her voice fell to a whisper. 'After what we shared...'

'What we shared was a bed,' he said coldly. 'And if you plan on detailing the more intimate aspects of our adventure for *WorldWeek*'s eager readers, I'd suggest you remember that every word you write about me will only make you look like the whore you are.'

The blood drained from her face. 'You can't really think...'

'Jaacov?'

The woman's voice was as soft as silk, but it silenced them both. She stood in the open door of the 'copter, a slender figure swathed in gold silk, her dark eyes fixed on Jake.

'Alana,' he whispered. He moved towards her quickly, a smile curving across his mouth. 'Alana, sweetheart, what are you doing here?'

The woman smiled, too, a smile that lit her beautiful face.

'How could I not come to you, Jaacov, when you have been away so long?'

Jake swept her into his arms and she wound her slender arms around his neck as he lifted her off the ground.

'Alana,' he said—and Dorian turned away.

'Oh, God,' she whispered.

Beside her, Kasmir smiled coldly. 'It is a sight to warm the heart, is it not, Miss Oliver?'

'Who—who is she?' Dorian asked unsteadily. But she knew. In her heart, she knew! 'Things will be different when we reach Kadar,' Jake had said...

'She is Alana Vadrovna—the betrothed of the *abdhan*.'

CHAPTER TWELVE

'YOU,' the grey-haired RBC-TV anchorman said, raising his glass of red wine in Dorian's direction, 'are one hell of a reporter.'

'Indeed she is.' The TNT-TV news commentator smiled. 'You've pulled off quite a coup, Miss Oliver.'

The leggy brunette from the Pyramid Network flashed her perfect white teeth. 'If you'd just give us a hint about the *real* Jack Alexander,' she said coyly, 'just a little colour for background information, of course...?'

The TNT-TV commentator shifted as close as the minuscule table in the bar of the Hotel Kadar would permit. 'Just some background material from an "unnamed source". We wouldn't violate your confidence.'

'No.' The brunette showed her white teeth again. 'You can count on that, Dorrie dear.'

'It's Dorian,' Dorian said.

The brunette's silken eyebrows lifted. 'Pardon?'

'My name.' Dorian's smile was all sweet innocence. She was tired of being buttered up by everybody from a stringer for *Der Spiegel* to the publisher of *The Times*. They, at least, had been less obvious than this trio. 'You keep calling me Dorrie—I'm called "Dorian". And I'm afraid you'll just have to wait until *WorldWeek* prints my article. I know my boss would be as livid as yours if I gave away an exclusive.'

Dorian's colleagues looked at each other. The fatherly gentleman from RBC frowned, announced his sentiments with a word that would have shocked his nightly viewers, and then belted down his third Scotch and soda of the evening.

'Well,' he said, 'this damned news blackout can't last forever.'

'It can last as long as Jack Alexander wants it to last,' the brunette said grumpily.

'You mean Jaacov Alexandrei,' the TNT-TV commentator said. 'Hell, now that he's ensconced in that medieval pile of stone up the road, he's sure as hell not Jack Alexander any more.'

'He's not even Jaacov Alexandrei,' the RBC anchor muttered. 'He's the *abdhan*, and he's not about to let us forget it.'

'He's not the *abdhan*,' Dorian said. They all looked up, startled, as if they'd forgotten her presence. 'He's still the *abdhazim*.' The three faces remained impassive. 'I mean, his cousin is still alive.'

'We know what you mean,' the brunette said with a condescending smile. 'What we don't know is why the bastard's clamped a lid on all information coming from the palace.' Her smile took on a crafty edge. 'But we suspect it might have something to do with you, sweetie, and that little sojourn in the wilderness you and he had.'

Dorian looked at the expectant faces. The false smiles were gone now, replaced by looks of sly speculation. She cleared her throat, then pushed back her chair.

'Well,' she said brightly, 'I think I'll call it a night.'

Was it her imagination, or did conversation pause as she made her way out of the hotel's café to the lobby? She couldn't tell any more; after a week of being her colleagues' centre of interest, Dorian had begun to feel mildly paranoid.

She stabbed her finger at the lift button. It had started the day she and Jake had been found. By the time the helicopter had whisked them to Kadar, the clutch of newspeople who'd been waiting at the Valley of the Two Suns had somehow been alerted to the fact that they were to be denied the story of the *abdhazim* and the reporter, so they'd been waiting to pounce on Dorian as she entered the hotel.

She'd begged off answering any questions, but her swollen eyes and trembling mouth had not gone unnoticed. And when word had come down from the palace that the *abdhazim* had decided that all news would from now on be cleared through his ministers the rumour mill had gone to work full tilt.

'What went on out there between you two?' people kept asking, although their nudges and winks made it clear that they really didn't require answers.

The lift doors opened and Dorian stepped inside. Walt had asked, too, during their first phone conversation, in words less subtle. It had been his very first question. Dorian had closed her eyes wearily and before she could answer the line had gone dead.

The lift shuddered to a stop and she stepped into the hotel corridor. Walt would be phoning soon for an update and she didn't want to miss his call. She was going to tell him what she'd been telling him for three days now.

She wanted to go home.

Not because of the rumours circulating around her; she was a big girl, and she could survive those. And not because she couldn't bear being in the same city as Jake. No. It was nothing as foolish as that.

The key trembled in her hand as she inserted it in the lock. She just—she just wanted to go home so that she could get started writing her story.

That made sense, didn't it? Everyone was waiting around to see if the *abdhan* would survive or if the *abdhazim* would be enthroned in his place, but she was weary of waiting. It wouldn't change her story: she had the goods on Jake Prince, and she'd tell it to the world as soon as she sat down at her word processor.

Her room was dark and quiet, and she sighed as she closed the door and tossed her room key on the desk. There was a tiny balcony, and she walked slowly to it and stepped outside.

Kadar lay softly lit and silent around her. Jake had said she would find the city with one foot in the past and one in the present, but he had not told her that she would also find it beautiful and exotic—but then, that depended on your perspective, didn't it? If you were virtually a prisoner inside the grey stone walls of the castle, as Jake was, exotic beauty didn't have much meaning.

Not that she felt the least bit of compassion for him. Why should she? Only a fool would feel compassion for a man like Jake Prince. Jake, or Jaacov Alexandrei, as he was now called, had no soul. And no heart.

And she had never loved him.

It had taken a lot of pain before she'd realised the truth; she'd wept into her pillow that first night in this room, wept until she'd had no tears left, but somewhere between the last fading star and the rise of the sun it had come to her.

Jake had hurt her pride, but not her heart. She had fallen in love with love, but not with him.

She'd been thrown into a dangerous yet romantic situation, with a handsome, virile man—a man to whom she'd been physically attracted, and the result had been inevitable. Who could blame her? Exhaustion, fear, the disorientation of having gone from a world she knew to one she'd never imagined had warped her perspective.

She had let him make love to her, and she'd romanticised it by telling herself it was love.

But it hadn't been love. It had been sex.

Dorian sighed as she stepped back into her room. How she could have let herself think, even for a moment, that she loved him was beyond her. What was there to love in a man like that? He was an arrogant, egotistical bastard who didn't care about anybody's feelings but his own, a man with an appetite for women and a hatred for reporters. As for the story he'd told her about the woman who'd betrayed him—who cared? Even if it were true, it didn't give him the right to treat people as he did, nor to treat her as he had.

He was, in short, an insolent barbarian who'd been given power by the fortunes of birth. He had no scruples about using people and then discarding them, but her turn was coming.

The pen, she thought with a little smile, was a mighty instrument indeed.

Jake could keep the lid on the news while she was here in Barovnia, but as soon as she reached the States the ball would be in her court. She was a reporter, and she had one hell of a story to tell. And, while she would not pepper the column she wrote with personal details, no matter what Jake thought, she would write about the man as he really was.

Selfish. Vain. Imperious. Unfeeling.

Jake Prince, A Scoundrel Among Men: A First-Person Account, by Dorian Oliver.

Yes, she thought as she brushed her teeth, that headline would do for a start. And the sooner she got started on writing the article that would accompany it, the better. Walt could fly someone in to replace her. He could——

The phone shrilled, and she snatched at it.

'New York's burning up with rumours, Blondie,' Walt said without preamble. She knew he was trying to talk fast enough to elude whoever might be monitoring the call. 'You should hear the stories going around about you and Alexander.'

Dorian closed her eyes. 'I can imagine.'

'Nope.' Walt chuckled. 'You can't. Some of them are pretty creative.'

'Why do I get the feeling you're not doing anything to stop them?'

He laughed. 'Hey, it's all free publicity, right? We're gonna outsell *Time* and *Newsweek* combined.'

'Walt?' She took a breath. 'I was thinking. Why don't I head back to New York tomorrow?'

'Now, Blondie, we've been through this. You hang in there until we see if the *abdhan* kicks the bucket.'

'But why? It won't change anything.'

'Of course it will. If your travelling companion becomes *abdhan*, your story will have even more kick.'

'I really don't see——'

'What's going on there, Oliver?' Walt's voice grew suspicious. 'You thinking of doing a deal with somebody else?'

'No. No, it's nothing like that. I just——'

'Good. Because you work for *WorldWeek*. You just remember that.'

'Walt.' Dorian stared at the receiver. 'Walt?'

The phone was dead. She sighed as she hung it up and then she rose slowly and walked to the balcony again.

All right. She could survive another few days. Maybe she'd start getting her notes together. Actually, there was nothing to stop her from starting the article now, while she cooled her heels in Kadar.

Her mouth hardened. Just wait until the world read the truth about Jaacov Alexandrei, who treated women like property, who took what he wanted and to hell with anyone else...

Who'd held her in his arms when she needed comforting, who'd made her cry out his name over and over during their long night together...

Dorian began to tremble. And all along, *all along*, the son of a bitch had been engaged to be married; he'd had a bride waiting for him in Kadar—one of his choosing, not simply one for the taking.

If only she hadn't seen Jake slip away from that charter flight! If only she hadn't followed him! She would have missed this story and what it was going to do for her career, but that would have been better than this, better than the pain that kept knifing through her heart...

A sob burst from her throat. Who was she kidding? She'd cried that first night and every night since, and, no matter how she concentrated on hating Jake, she couldn't stop wanting him.

She spun away from the balcony, hurried into the bedroom, and threw open the wardrobe door. Her career was important, but not as important as her sanity. She had to get control of her life again, and she could not do that here, in a place where Jake Prince was Emperor of the World. She was going back to New York, where she belonged, and if Walt Hemple didn't like it he could just go to hell.

It turned out to be easy to slip out of the hotel unnoticed. Her fellow journalists had turned the café into a clubhouse, which meant that the lobby was deserted when Dorian stepped from the lift. The taxi she'd called was waiting just outside.

'The airport, please.'

'Airport, *da*,' the driver said, and with the careless disregard for speed limits of taxi drivers everywhere he wove through the quiet streets of the city, on to the one main highway, and delivered her with more than an hour to spare before the late-night flight to New York.

She began to feel better as soon as she entered the terminal. She would be home soon, among all the things that were familiar, and what had happened to her in this country would be nothing but a memory.

Her steps faltered as she approached the ticket counter. Jake would be a memory, too. How long would it take to purge her thoughts of him? A month? A year?

A lifetime ...

'*Bobska*?'

She looked up, startled. The ticket clerk was smiling pleasantly. Dorian smiled in return.

'Sorry. One-way to New York.' Dorian pushed her credit card across the counter. 'Charge it, please.'

'You have luggage, miss?'

'No. Just a bag.'

'Passport?'

Dorian nodded. 'Yes. Here it is.'

The woman took the little blue booklet and opened it. Her face creased in a frown. After a moment Dorian cleared her throat.

'Is there a problem?'

The clerk looked up. 'Is no entry stamp, miss.'

'No entry . . .' Dorian blew out her breath. How could there be an entry stamp, when she had not entered the country through Customs? 'No,' she said, 'no, there isn't. But I came in legally, I assure you.'

The clerk frowned again. 'Must be stamp, miss.'

'I didn't come in the usual way. I—I . . .' She bit down on her lip. How could she explain? Someone had done a rough translation of the local Press's coverage of Jake's unorthodox entry into Barovnia; she had not been mentioned. The clerk's English was limited and Dorian's Barovnian non-existent. Explaining would take half the night, by which time the plane would have left.

'Look, is there a supervisor around? A supervisor. Someone in charge.' Dorian leaned forward. 'Don't you have a boss?' she asked desperately.

'A boss!' The clerk smiled. 'You wait, please.'

She waited five minutes, then ten, and when she was almost ready to stamp her feet with frustration a man came strolling out from an office down the hall.

'How do you do?' Dorian said with a fixed smile. 'My name is Dorian Oliver, and——'

'The reporter?'

Her smiled wavered a little. Had the rumours spread outside the circle of reporters? Had she become a household name among the Barovnians, too?

'Yes,' she said briskly, 'that's right. There's a slight problem with my passport, but I thought, if you'd just phone my Embassy. I know it's late, but I'm sure there's an emergency number, and——'

'There is no problem, miss.'

Dorian let out her breath. 'Well, that's good news.'

'Please.' He smiled and inclined his head. 'If you'll just come into my office and make yourself comfortable——'

'But my plane...' Her gaze flew to the wall clock as he took her arm and led her down the hall. 'It leaves in three quarters of an hour.'

'Make yourself at home, please, Miss Oliver. I'll take care of the problem immediately.'

'But...'

The door swung shut after him. Dorian stared at it, and then she stalked across the room and sank down on an institutional plastic sofa.

Now what? She'd heard endless stories from foreign correspondents about how many hours, if not days, it could take to get through red tape, especially in out-of-the-way little countries.

She pushed back her sleeve and looked at her watch. Ten more minutes had slipped by.

'Come on,' she said through her teeth, 'come on!'

Five minutes passed, and then five more, and finally Dorian slapped her hands on her knees and stood up.

'OK,' she said grimly, 'enough is enough!' She stalked to the door and grabbed the handle—but it wouldn't turn. Her brow creased; she twisted it again and again. 'Hey!' Her voice rose. 'Hey! Open this door, will you?' She waited, but there was only silence. 'Do you hear me?' Furiously, she pounded both fists on the door. 'You open this door right now,' she yelled, 'or I'll—I'll...'

She fell back as the door swung open. 'Or you'll what?' Jake said coldly.

For a moment she was too stunned to speak. Then, gradually, she felt her brain begin to function again.

'Jake,' she whispered. 'What—what are you doing here?'

He stepped into the room and slammed the door behind him. 'I'm not the one answering questions, Dorian. You are.'

'Did—did that foolish man call you? I didn't ask him to do that; I asked him to call——'

'The Embassy. Yes. I know.'

'Then why did he call you?' Her chin lifted. 'Was my name on a list? Are you trying to stop reporters from leaving the country?'

He strode past her, leaned back against the desk, and folded his arms across his chest.

'Why are you sneaking out of Barovnia in the middle of the night?'

Colour striped her cheeks. 'I am not sneaking out in the middle of the night.'

Jake crossed his feet at the ankles. 'It's almost one a.m. If that's not the middle of the night, what is it?'

Her chin lifted in defiance. 'Early morning.'

A quick, cool smile flashed across his face. 'I'd almost forgotten how clever you are with words, Dorian. Now that we've done with the pleasantries, perhaps you'll answer my question. Why are you leaving Barovnia?'

She stared at him. 'I don't have to answer that.'

'No,' he said, nodding his head, 'no, you don't. You can just sit here until the sun comes up, and——'

'I'll have missed my plane by then.'

He shrugged lazily. 'There'll be another.'

But not until midday, she thought in sudden desperation. And I can't stay here any longer, Jake, I can't...

'I can't,' she said, a little breathlessly. 'My—my boss wants me in New York immediately.'

Jake's teeth flashed in a quick smile. 'Your boss told you to stay here until your job was finished. I may not have the phrasing exactly right, but——'

'You *have* been tapping my phone!'

'Why are you running away, Dorian?'

Their eyes met. 'I'm not.'

Jake reached into his pocket and held out her passport. 'And why,' he asked softly, 'are you trying to use this when you know it's illegal?'

Dorian glared at him. 'My passport isn't illegal.'

'Really? That's not what Mr Sojac tells me. He says you have no entry stamp.'

'Of course I haven't. How could I, when I never entered the country through Customs?'

'No.' His eyes grew cold and hard. 'You never entered to the applause of your colleagues, either, but then, it was just your hard luck that I managed to spoil your plans.'

She stared at him, her breasts rising and falling with the rapidity of her breathing. She could feel her anger slipping away; it was being replaced by bleak despair, but she mustn't let that happen.

So what if he thought she'd betrayed him? The truth was that *he* had betrayed her, and in the cruellest sort of way. She had to keep remembering that, remembering how she despised him...

'Jake.' She cleared her throat. 'Please. Don't do this.'

'Don't do what?' He opened the little blue book and peered into it, leafing idly through the pages as if he might come across something interesting. 'What a pity,' he said. 'You don't seem to have done very much travelling.' He looked at her. 'Don't you like to travel?'

'Dammit, Jake——'

'But then, of course, travel is expensive.' He frowned as he flicked the passport shut. 'Well, not to worry. Now that you're about to become a hotshot columnist, your boss will send you anywhere you want to go. The Far East. South America. Paris, London.' His face darkened. 'Of course, you want to be sure he doesn't try to send you where you're not welcome.'

'What is it, Jake? Do you want me to beg?' Her voice was steady, but her hand shook as she held it out to him. 'If you've any decency at all, you'll give me my——'

'Decency.' His voice caressed the word. 'And what would you know of decency, Dorian?'

'Give me my passport!'

He smiled coolly. 'If you want it that badly, come and get it.'

'Jake, dammit!' Dorian slammed her hand against the desk. 'This isn't a game!'

'Sure it is. And you play games so well. Don't you want to play another?'

'You—you——' A word burst from her lips as she flew across the room. 'Give me that!' she demanded.

Jake laughed as he raised the passport over his head. 'Give you what? This?'

Tears rose in her eyes. 'I hate you, Jake Prince,' she panted as she stretched for the little blue booklet. 'Damn you to hell!'

'No,' he said, and suddenly he wasn't laughing any more, 'no, Dorian, you can't damn me to hell.' He caught her wrists in his hands, spun her around, and backed her against the desk. 'You already did that once, you see; you don't get a second chance.'

Her breath sobbed in and out of her lungs as she struggled against him. 'Let go of me, Jake! I swear, if you don't, I'll—I'll——'

'You'll what? Call the cops? The militia? The king?' He laughed. 'Don't waste your time, Dorian. I *am* the cops. And the militia. And the king, in effect, remember? I'm all those things—and I'm also the man you betrayed.'

'*I* betrayed *you*? That's a laugh.'

'You're damned right you betrayed me.' He let go of her wrists and clasped her shoulders in his hands. 'You set me up. You fed me little titbits of sex and sweet compassion, so you could lead me like a lamb to the slaughter.'

'No. That's not true.'

'Are you trying to pretend you didn't send a telegram to *World Week*?'

'I was only doing my job. But you——'

'And what a job you did,' he said coldly. 'Setting me up for the cameras——'

'That's a lie!' Angry tears rose in her eyes and she swiped them away with her hand. 'I tried to warn you——'

'When, Dorian? Just tell me that!'

'I *did* try! I tried to tell you during the night, when you awakened me. And——'

'Yes.' Jake shifted his weight, so that his body brushed lightly against hers. 'I remember waking you. I remember it very clearly.'

She remembered too, oh, yes, she remembered. His kisses. His whispers. The feel of his hands and his mouth...

'And—and then the next morning,' she said quickly. 'I kept saying I said I had to talk to you. I was going to tell you about the telegram I'd sent.'

'So what? Maybe you'd decided you'd made a mistake, calling for the reserves. Hell, you'd drawn stuff out of me that would make for quite a story. Keeping it an exclusive would have made it more valuable.'

Dorian stared at him. 'You're a fine one to talk,' she whispered. 'You—you used me, Jake. I was just—I was a toy, something to play with...'

Her throat constricted. What was the point in this? Jake hated her, and she—she hated him. Nothing they could say would change that, and if it was hard to stand this close to him without reaching out and trying to smooth away the tiny lines at the corners of his mouth and eyes it was only because—because...

Her heart fell. It was because she loved him, and she always would, despite what he'd done to her. If there was a special place in hell for a man who'd treated a woman as Jake had treated her, then there had to be a place there, too, for a woman foolish enough to go on loving such a man.

Tears rose in her eyes, and she turned her head away.

'Please,' she said in a choked whisper, 'let me go home.'

'Why? So you can get back to New York and write your story? What are you going to call it, *The Lady and The Barbarian*?'

'No. I—I won't write anything like that. I'll just—I'll write about—about a man who—who...'

She fell silent. She would not write this story at all, she thought, and the realisation came as no great surprise. Perhaps she'd known it all along. She would never write about Jake. How could she, when no matter what she said or how she said it she would violate not just his privacy, but the precious time they'd shared?

Jake clasped her chin and forced her to look at him. 'About a man who what? What's your story for *WorldWeek* going to be about?'

Dorian took a deep breath. 'Nothing. There'll be nothing in the magazine.'

'I see.' He glared at her. 'So you sold out to the highest bidder. Who was it, Dorian? American TV? The British penny papers? I hear *Stern* pays damned well.' He jerked her head up. 'Who'd you sell your soul to?'

'No one.' She met his eyes. 'I'm not going to write anything at all. I know you don't believe me——'

'You're right, I don't.'

'So I'll sign a release, or whatever it is you call it. Just have your lawyers send it to me——'

She cried out as his hands slipped to her shoulders and he half lifted her to her toes.

'What kind of fool do you take me for? You go off to New York, and it's too late for me to do anything. No, Dorian, you're going to have to do a lot better than that.'

'What, then?' The tears she'd tried so hard to stop began to trickle down her cheeks. 'What do you want from me, Jake? What can I do to prove that—that I'd sooner die than hurt you?'

The admission hung between them, drifting in the air like smoke from a dying fire. Dorian wanted to call the words back, but it was too late. Jake's hands slid from her shoulders to curve lightly around her face.

'I'll tell you what you can do,' he said, his voice suddenly soft and gentle. 'You can kiss me.'

'No. Jake, no. Don't. I don't—I can't...'

He bent his head and brushed his mouth lightly over hers. It was a soft, gentle kiss, and she tried to turn away from it, but he held her fast, his lips moving over hers tenderly, sweetly, and, despite her determination not to reveal herself to him more than she already had, she gave a little sob and swayed towards him. Her arms linked around his neck as he gathered her to him, and she returned his kiss with the same tenderness and passion.

They stayed that way for a long, long time, lost in each other's arms, and then, finally, Jake drew back.

'Did you really think I'd let you leave Barovnia so easily?' he asked softly.

Dorian leaned her forehead against his chest. 'Why are you doing this?' she asked in a broken whisper.

'Because I want to hear you admit the truth.' He held her from him and looked into her eyes. 'You're in love with me.'

Her eyes filled with tears. 'This isn't fair,' she whispered. 'You have to leave me something, Jake. My pride, at least.'

He smiled. 'Why should I, kitten? You haven't left me anything but days and nights of anguish.'

'Don't.' She sighed as he drew her against his heart. 'Don't lie to me. There's no reason.'

'You're right, there isn't. That's why I'm going to tell you the truth.' He took her face in his hands and kissed her mouth. 'I love you, kitten.'

Wild joy filled her heart—but then she remembered.

'No,' she whispered. 'You don't.'

'Don't I?'

Dorian closed her eyes. 'I've seen Alana, remember?'

Jake's brows rose. 'Alana?'

She looked at him. 'Yes. And if you're going to tell me that a prerogative of royalty is—is having both a wife and a mistress, I'm not interested.'

He smiled. 'That's a very old-fashioned notion, kitten.'

Her mouth trembled. 'Didn't I ever tell you, Jake? I'm an old-fashioned girl.'

'Very well.' He let go of her, reached into his pocket, and held out her passport. 'Go on,' he said, 'take it. It belongs to you.'

Well, what had she expected? He was the *abdhazim* and Alana was the bride he'd chosen. Carefully, eyes downcast so that he would not see the tell-tale gleam of tears on her lashes, Dorian took the passport from him.

'Thank you.'

'You're welcome. What are you going to do with that, now that you've got it?'

Dorian looked up. 'You know what I'm going to do with it. I'm going to go back to the States.'

He nodded. 'That's a good idea. I'll be doing the same thing in another few weeks, when my cousin's fully able to resume normal activities.'

'The *abdhan*'s all right, then?'

'Yes.'

She smiled tremulously. 'I'm glad,' she whispered. 'Now you won't have to be *abdhan*. You can go back to your old life.'

Smiling, he reached out and touched her hair. 'Well, with some modifications, I suppose. I've agreed to spend part of the year here, to help Seref modernise our country.'

'Good. I mean, I know that's important to you.'

'And then, there's my marriage.'

Dorian swallowed past the lump in her throat. 'Yes. Your marriage.' She turned away. 'I wish you only the best, of course.'

'Of course.' His voice was solemn. 'Well. I suppose I'd better get back to my people. When I got the call that you were trying to leave, we'd just got word of Seref's recovery. The celebration is still going on.'

She nodded. Don't cry, she warned herself fiercely, as he started to turn away, don't you dare cry!

'But I suppose I should warn you, though...'

'Warn me?'

'Yes.' Jake looked at her. 'They won't accept your passport.'

She blinked. 'What do you mean?'

'Well, it's not stamped.' He frowned, but she could see the laughter in his eyes. 'You're in the country illegally, and that's a serious offence.'

'But—but we've been through all this! I *am* here legally!'

He shook his head. 'Nope,' he said, leaning back against the door and folding his arms over his chest, 'you're not. And your passport lists you as Dorian Oliver.'

'Of course it does. That's my name!'

He smiled lazily. 'No, it isn't. Your name is Dorian Alexander. Or Dorian Alexandrei.' He laughed. 'Or maybe even Dorian Prince.'

A tremor went through her. 'Jake. What are you talking about?'

He reached for her and drew her to him. 'We're married, kitten. You're my wife.'

'No. No, I'm not. It wasn't legal. You said so yourself.'

A sly smile tugged at the corners of his mouth. 'I lied.'

'What?'

'Well, what else was I going to do? You had to agree to that ceremony, or it would have been the end of the line.' He tilted her face to his. 'Besides, when a man finds love, he'll do anything to keep it.' His smile became a grin. 'Even get married.'

'Married?' she whispered. 'We're really married?'

He laughed softly. 'Don't look so upset, darling. We can take our vows again, if you like, in a proper setting with all the trimmings.'

'But—but what about Alana?'

Jake nuzzled her throat. 'What about her?'

'Well, you can't marry the both of us, not even in Barovnia.' She frowned and the tip of her tongue touched her lip. 'Can you?'

'Not unless I want Seref to take me out and shoot me.'

Dorian stared at him. 'Seref?'

'Alana is just what Kasmir said she was, sweetheart. She's the betrothed of the *abdhan*. The three of us grew up together, but it's been special between the two of them for a long, long time.' He smiled. 'I'm going to warn Seref that he and Alana had better have enough little princes and princesses so I never have to worry about becoming the *abdhan* again.'

'Oh, Jake. I thought...' She shook her head. 'Why did you let me think we were going to the Valley of the Two Suns?'

Jake's mouth twisted. 'I suppose—I suppose I didn't trust you. I was going to explain...'

'But there wasn't time.'

He nodded. 'Exactly. Can you forgive me?'

Dorian smiled. 'I'll forgive you,' she whispered, 'if you forgive me.'

He kissed her, and she sighed. 'That last night, though—I kept hoping you'd tell me the truth about yourself, but you didn't.'

'I wanted to. But if anyone in camp had recognised me, all bets were off. They might have held us for ransom; they might have decided to slit our throats.' He gathered her tightly into his arms. 'It was a burden I couldn't share with you, kitten. Do you see?'

She nestled into his embrace. 'What I see,' she said softly, 'is that you've protected me from the minute we met.'

'And I'll go on doing it for the rest of my life, if you'll let me.'

He kissed her deeply. After a long time Dorian stirred.

'Have you forgotten, my *abdhazim*, that your people are waiting for you?'

Jake swung her up into his arms. 'How do you feel about keeping to the old ways, sweetheart?'

Dorian smiled. 'You mean, you want me to quit *World Week*?'

'No.' He took a deep breath. 'No, love, I wouldn't ask that of you.'

'But you can,' she said softly. 'You see, I'd much rather be at my husband's side than at my desk in New York.'

'You really are an old-fashioned girl,' he said, smiling. 'Who would have dreamed it?'

She linked her arms around his neck. 'But I'd never agree to walk ten paces to the rear of my husband.'

'No,' Jake said. His smile broadened. 'I didn't think you would.'

'And I'd never promise to remain mute.'

'The custom I had in mind is a little bit different, kitten. It's one that says that the *abdhazim* brings his bride to his castle and shows her to his people, so they can all see how beautiful she is.'

'Ah. Well, that sounds lovely.'

Jake kissed her. 'And then,' he whispered, 'he takes her to his rooms, and he makes love to her until the sun is high in the sky.'

Dorian sighed and laid her head against his shoulder.

'Sometimes,' she said softly, 'the old ways are very definitely the best.'

FLYAWAY VACATION SWEEPSTAKES!

This month's destination:

Glamorous LAS VEGAS!

Are you the lucky person who will win a free trip to Las Vegas? Think how much fun it would be to visit world-famous casinos... to see star-studded shows...to enjoy round-the-clock action in the city that never sleeps!

The facing page contains two Official Entry Coupons, as does each of the other books you received this shipment. Complete and return all the entry coupons—**the more times you enter, the better your chances of winning!**

Then keep your fingers crossed, because you'll find out by August 15, 1995 if you're the winner! If you are, here's what you'll get:

- Round-trip airfare for two to exciting Las Vegas!
- 4 days/3 nights at a fabulous first-class hotel!
- $500.00 pocket money for meals and entertainment!

Remember: The more times you enter, the better your chances of winning!*

*NO PURCHASE OR OBLIGATION TO CONTINUE BEING A SUBSCRIBER NECESSARY TO ENTER. SEE REVERSE SIDE OF ANY ENTRY COUPON FOR ALTERNATIVE MEANS OF ENTRY.

VLV KAL

FLYAWAY VACATION
SWEEPSTAKES

OFFICIAL ENTRY COUPON

This entry must be received by: JULY 30, 1995
This month's winner will be notified by: AUGUST 15, 1995
Trip must be taken between: SEPTEMBER 30, 1995-SEPTEMBER 30, 1996

YES, I want to win a vacation for two in Las Vegas. I understand the prize includes round-trip airfare, first-class hotel and $500.00 spending money. Please let me know if I'm the winner!

Name_____

Address _____Apt. _____

City   State/Prov.   Zip/Postal Code

Account #_____

Return entry with invoice in reply envelope.

© 1995 HARLEQUIN ENTERPRISES LTD.   CLV KAL

OFFICIAL RULES
FLYAWAY VACATION SWEEPSTAKES 3449
NO PURCHASE OR OBLIGATION NECESSARY

Three Harlequin Reader Service 1995 shipments will contain respectively, coupons for entry into three different prize drawings, one for a trip for two to San Francisco, another for a trip for two to Las Vegas and the third for a trip for two to Orlando, Florida. To enter any drawing using an Entry Coupon, simply complete and mail according to directions.

There is no obligation to continue using the Reader Service to enter and be eligible for any prize drawing. You may also enter any drawing by hand printing the words "Flyaway Vacation," your name and address on a 3"x5" card and the destination of the prize you wish that entry to be considered for (i.e., San Francisco trip, Las Vegas trip or Orlando trip). Send your 3"x5" entries via first-class mail (limit: one entry per envelope) to: Flyaway Vacation Sweepstakes 3449, c/o Prize Destination you wish that entry to be considered for, P.O. Box 1315, Buffalo, NY 14269-1315, USA or P.O. Box 610, Fort Erie, Ontario L2A 5X3, Canada.

To be eligible for the San Francisco trip, entries must be received by 5/30/95; for the Las Vegas trip, 7/30/95; and for the Orlando trip, 9/30/95.

Winners will be determined in random drawings conducted under the supervision of D.L. Blair, Inc., an independent judging organization whose decisions are final, from among all eligible entries received for that drawing. San Francisco trip prize includes round-trip airfare for two, 4-day/3-night weekend accommodations at a first-class hotel, and $500 in cash (trip must be taken between 7/30/95—7/30/96, approximate prize value—$3,500); Las Vegas trip includes round-trip airfare for two, 4-day/3-night weekend accommodations at a first-class hotel, and $500 in cash (trip must be taken between 9/30/95—9/30/96, approximate prize value—$3,500); Orlando trip includes round-trip airfare for two, 4-day/3-night weekend accommodations at a first-class hotel, and $500 in cash (trip must be taken between 11/30/95—11/30/96, approximate prize value—$3,500). All travelers must sign and return a Release of Liability prior to travel. Hotel accommodations and flights are subject to accommodation and schedule availability. Sweepstakes open to residents of the U.S. (except Puerto Rico) and Canada, 18 years of age or older. Employees and immediate family members of Harlequin Enterprises, Ltd., D.L. Blair, Inc., their affiliates, subsidiaries and all other agencies, entities and persons connected with the use, marketing or conduct of this sweepstakes are not eligible. Odds of winning a prize are dependent upon the number of eligible entries received for that drawing. Prize drawing and winner notification for each drawing will occur no later than 15 days after deadline for entry eligibility for that drawing. Limit: one prize to an individual, family or organization. All applicable laws and regulations apply. Sweepstakes offer void wherever prohibited by law. Any litigation within the province of Quebec respecting the conduct and awarding of the prizes in this sweepstakes must be submitted to the Regles des loteries et Courses du Quebec. In order to win a prize, residents of Canada will be required to correctly answer a time-limited arithmetical skill-testing question. Value of prizes are in U.S. currency.

Winners will be obligated to sign and return an Affidavit of Eligibility within 30 days of notification. In the event of noncompliance within this time period, prize may not be awarded. If any prize or prize notification is returned as undeliverable, that prize will not be awarded. By acceptance of a prize, winner consents to use of his/her name, photograph or other likeness for purposes of advertising, trade and promotion on behalf of Harlequin Enterprises, Ltd., without further compensation, unless prohibited by law.

For the names of prizewinners (available after 12/31/95), send a self-addressed, stamped envelope to: Flyaway Vacation Sweepstakes 3449 Winners, P.O. Box 4200, Blair, NE 68009.

RVC KAL